PRAISE FOR SNOWSPELLED

With its unique

SNOWSPELLED is c

magic. Stephanie Bu

can't wait to see wh

sequel!

— ILONA ANDREWS, #1 NEW YORK TIMES BESTSELLING AUTHOR OF THE KATE DANIELS SERIES AND THE HIDDEN LEGACY SERIES

A squee-filled, can't-stop-smiling delight.

— STARSHIP SOFA

Sweet, funny, clever and romantic.

— ROSALYN EVES, AUTHOR OF BLOOD ROSE REBELLION

SNOWSPELLED

Volume One of The Harwood Spellbook

STEPHANIE BURGIS

Five Fathoms Press

ISBN 978-1-9997254-0-2

Five Fathoms Press

DEDICATION

For Vickie Ruggiero: Sister of the Fork, fellow breakfast adventurer, Skype Book Club partner, and more. Here's to the next 28 years of friendship!

I

Of course, a sensible woman would never have accepted the invitation in the first place.

To attend a week-long house party filled with bickering gentleman magicians, ruthlessly cutthroat lady politicians, and worst of all, my own infuriating ex-fiancé? Scarcely two months after I had scandalized all of our most intimate friends by jilting him?

Utter madness. And anyone would have seen that immediately ... except for my incurably romantic sister-in-law.

Unfortunately, Amy saw the invitation pop into mid-air beside me as we sat *en famille* at the breakfast table that morning. She watched with bright interest as I crumpled it up a moment later in disgust ... and then she dashed around the table, with surprising agility despite her interesting condition, to snatch the ball of paper from my hands before I could toss it into the blazing fire where it belonged.

Naturally, I lunged to retrieve it. But I was too late.

The moment she smoothed it out enough to read the details, her eyes lit up with near-fanatical ardor. "Oh, *yes*,

Cassandra, we *must* go! Just think: you will finally see Wrexham again!"

"I know," I said through gritted teeth. "That is exactly why we are going to refuse it!"

"Now, love..." Her eyes widened, and she gave me her most innocent look ... which put me on guard immediately.

Kind-hearted, loyal, and *adorable* are all phrases that may apply very well to my brother's wife; *innocent* is not one of them, and never has been.

She had, after all, been my mother's final and most promising political protégée.

"I should think," she said now, as if idly, "that you would wish to show everyone how little notice you take of any gossip. After all, if we refuse this invitation, you know everyone will say it was because you were too afraid to see Wrexham again."

My teeth ground together. "I am *not* afraid of seeing Wrexham."

"Well, *I* know that," Amy said, looking as smug as a cat licking up fresh cream. "But does *he*?"

Well. It isn't that I don't know when I'm being managed. But there are some possibilities that cannot be borne. And the thought of my ex-fiancé's dark eyebrows rising in his most fiendishly supercilious look at the news of my cowardly refusal...

I drummed my fingers against the table, searching for a way out.

Behind my brother's outspread newspaper, an apparently disembodied voice spoke. "Better leave early," my brother said. "It's meant to snow next week, according to the weather wizards."

Amy sat back, smiling and resting her hands on her rounded belly...

And that was how the three of us ended up rattling through the elven dales in mid-winter, with the first flakes of snow falling around our carriage.

Poor Amy stopped chattering half an hour into our journey, her pretty face setting into pained lines and her dark brown skin taking on a grayish hue. As I watched her, my toes tapped once, twice, and then a third time beneath my skirts.

I forced myself to look away.

The carriage bumped over a particularly large rock, and a tiny, muffled squeak escaped from Amy's lips. My fingers clenched. All it would take was the simplest little spell to relieve her misery ... if only a competent, *functioning* magician sat beside her.

No matter how hard I tried, I could never manage a full day without a reminder of my failure.

Beside me, Amy breathed deeply and leaned back against the seat.

All the taxes had been paid on our carriage, the glowing seal stamped proudly on its side less than a month earlier, so the trolls who guarded these dales stood unmoving in the falling snow, letting us drive past without incident. As the wintry sun lowered in the sky and the snow thickened, their massive, looming figures took on the indistinct shapes of rugged, rocky green hills ... at least, until another carriage turned onto the road behind us and the closest troll swung into lumbering motion, its massive, moss-covered arms swinging by its sides.

I craned to look back through the window, grateful for the distraction, but the swirling snow obscured the scene behind us.

"Idiots," said my brother calmly. "Thought they could

get away with their old tax seal till the end of the year, probably."

"They aren't being foolish and resisting, are they?" Amy cracked her eyes open, frowning.

"Oh, no, they're going quietly enough." Jonathan snorted, crossing one leg over another. "But I shouldn't fancy having *my* carriage swung about in the grip of a troll all the way to the local toll station. Would you?"

"Ugh —!" Amy's face crumpled. She lifted one gloved hand to her lips and squeezed her eyes tightly shut.

"Think of ginger root," I told her hastily, as I gave her husband a narrow-eyed look. "And dry biscuits. And —"

"No food, please." Her voice was muffled by her hand. "Not while I'm still thinking of swinging carriages."

"Sorry, love." Jonathan looked chagrined. "We can't be far from Cosgrave Manor now. If this dashed snow would only clear up a bit... It wasn't even supposed to start snowing for two or three more days!"

But the too-early snowfall ignored its orders, thickening more and more until our progress had been slowed to a near-walk. It was nearly another hour before we finally arrived at our destination. Amy was positively green by then, her face pinched tight, and I was vibrating like a maddened dog with frustration.

The simplest, smallest little spell...

It would have been so easy to whisk her nausea away only four months earlier. But of course she hadn't needed any of my spellcraft then, and now that she did...

I stalked out of the carriage at Cosgrave Manor with my spine stiff and my skirts swishing about me, ready to rip to verbal shreds anyone rash enough to get between me and the privacy of my guest bedroom. There, I could let out all of my useless rage and then compose myself before facing any crowded drawing rooms or inane small talk...

...Or, worst of all, my ex-fiancé. I couldn't face him now. Not yet.

I should never have agreed to come here in the first place.

But the house was already in an uproar when we stepped into it.

"Oh, for goodness' sake!" Lady Cosgrave stood in the front hall with one hand pressed dramatically to her forehead, while her husband and two other men I recognized as competent magicians pulled on greatcoats and hats with grim frustration on their faces. Two more of Angland's finest politicians stood beyond our hostess, dressed in their finest fairy-silks, waving their glittering, elven-made fans in disapproval, and wearing their most supercilious expressions as they watched their husbands prepare themselves for the wintry weather. These ladies were dressed to rule, not for outdoor management, and this was clearly not the entertainment they had planned.

"Just *find* them, please," Lady Cosgrave told her own husband, in a tone that had been strained to breaking point. "And when I get my hands on that child — ah!" She broke off as she finally spotted us standing in the doorway of the foyer. "Amy! And Mr. Harwood, of course, and Cassandra, too. How wonderful to see you all. But —"

"But what's amiss, Honoria?" Amy hurried forward to take her hands. Anyone who didn't know my sister-in-law well would never guess at how ill she must still be feeling even now that we were out of the carriage — but, being Amy, her attention was focused purely on our hostess and her expression was filled with genuine concern. "Have we come at a poor moment?"

"Oh, no, hardly. In fact..." Lady Cosgrave sighed and traded glances with the other two members of the Boudiccate who stood behind her. "Well," she said, "we could certainly use another member for our search party. We've just had a spelled message to alert us that my young cousin's party has been lost in the snow. She was traveling with a group of friends whose carriage was confiscated — can you believe that anyone could be so foolish as to forget to pay their taxes before such a journey, at this time of year? — and the tyrants at the toll station turned them out to find their way here without a single gentleman to accompany them on their way."

"By foot in this weather? Without a magician in the party?" Jonathan raised his eyebrows. "Good Lord."

"I know you can't help us with the magical aspect, Mr. Harwood," Lady Cosgrave said. "But hardly anyone is here yet to help because of this dreadful snowstorm. So if you wouldn't mind being a pair of extra eyes for the search..."

Amy only gave the slightest fraction of a wince. But it was enough.

"My brother will be far too busy to help," I told our hostess firmly. "Amy needs rest after our journey, Honoria, even if she doesn't wish to admit it. She needs to lie down and be looked after for a good hour now, and Jonathan should be the one to look after her, for all of our sakes. But I can take his place, I promise you."

"You?" Her eyebrows arched. "But, my dear..."

"*Cassandra*!" Amy said. "You know —!"

"You needn't worry," I told them both with a snap in my voice. "I won't be fool enough to cast any spells of my own." I might still be battling despair every day, but I wasn't — anymore — at that bleak point where I'd consider risking my life for that brief satisfaction. "But Jonathan couldn't have cast any in the first place, could he? So why shouldn't I take his place in this search party, if no magic's required for it?"

Jonathan snorted, and Lady Cosgrave's eyebrows rose even higher, but it was my sister-in-law, of course, who was officially the head of my family ... and there were very few people who knew me as well as she did, nowadays. So after looking into my eyes for a long, fraught moment, Amy blew out her breath. "Very well," she said. "But please: *be careful.*"

"Of course," I said, and gave her a wry smile. "Haven't I spent the last few months learning how to do just that?"

Amy would never be so disloyal as to deliver any retort where outsiders could overhear it. But her expression spoke the words almost as clearly as Jonathan whispered them a moment later, in the ancient Densk that he and I had used for years as a secret language, as he arranged his heavy greatcoat around the shoulders of my hooded pelisse and I stepped into a pair of Lady Cosgrave's own tall, fur-lined boots:

"That's exactly what worries us."

My family loved me. And I was more grateful than words could ever acknowledge for their protection. It would not even be too gross an overstatement to say that it had saved me after the events of four months earlier.

But as Lord Cosgrave pushed open the front door and the four members of our search party stepped out from the safety of the heated manor house into the wild and whirling snow, I finally tasted something I hadn't experienced in months of being cosseted and consoled for my loss at every turn:

Freedom.

Cold, bracing air filled my lungs. Jonathan's greatcoat draped me in warmth.

I stepped forward and smiled as snow kissed my cheeks.

"Miss Harwood." Lord Cosgrave cleared his throat as he passed me a lantern. "If you wouldn't mind..."

"Of course." My smile tightened. The other men avoided my eyes.

I knew them all, of course. I'd been the only woman in a group of men more times than I could count in my adult life, until all lingering discomfort — at least on my part — had worn away entirely. There was a time when every magician in the country had known my name after I'd first fought my way into their ranks, aided by the power of my own family name and by Jonathan and Amy's staunch support. The newspapers, naturally, had found it all hilarious: *The lady who thought she was a magician.*

But if Jonathan could bear the caricatures they'd done of us — *the Harwood Horrors; siblings born to the wrong sexes?* — so could I. And I'd won the grudging respect of my peers, by the end.

So they all knew exactly how I'd fallen four months earlier.

It took every ounce of my strength to stand still now, with my chin held high and a cool expression stitched onto my face, as Lord Cosgrave moved in a slow circle around me, chanting the spell of protection from the elements.

It was only what he would have done for Jonathan, I reminded myself — and Jonathan had lived all his life without the ability to work magic. Not every man could do spellwork, of course, even in our elite cohort, just as I couldn't possibly have been the first woman to be born with that natural ability. I was only the first to be bold enough, brash enough and — most of all — lucky enough, in our modern era, to finally break free of the roles we'd all been assigned centuries earlier, and win a public space for myself that others might follow.

But Jonathan was different.

I would never know the full truth of how my brother's school years had gone — although I had my suspicions — but I knew exactly how he interacted with the other men of our cohort now. If it were Jonathan standing here in my place, they would all have been laughing as the spell was cast for his protection, and he'd have been making the most jovial remarks of all as the four of them grinned at each other in utterly complicit masculine conviviality.

Now, the soft hiss of the snow was the only sound outside the tightly-closed-up house apart from Lord Cosgrave's monotonous chanting. My jaw tightened as he mispronounced the second word in a row, but I restrained myself, with an effort, from correcting him. As he finally completed the circle, the spell clicked shut, and a warm, dry circle formed around me.

... Almost dry, anyway. There was a sliver of a leak just behind my neck. Icy water trickled down my hood.

I could have told him exactly how to re-cast the spell with more clarity and precision, to avoid any such leaks in the future.

Five months earlier, I could have shown him myself.

Now, I nodded stiffly and held up the lantern, straining to be off. "Has a tracking spell already been set on this?"

"Ah..." Lord Cosgrave's eyebrows beetled downwards. "We don't have Miss Fennell's exact direction, so —"

"Not for her, for the *house*," I said. "If I should get turned around in the snow."

He blinked, and I could actually *see* him remembering: unlike the rest of them, I couldn't cast my own way home. "Oh. Right-o," he said, and coughed.

It would have helped by an infinite amount if any of the men around me had only sniggered or had the decency to look even slightly contemptuous of my weakness.

The pity that the three of them oozed instead, as they unanimously averted their eyes from my figure, was thick enough to incite justifiable homicide. My fingers tightened around my lantern. At least Wrexham wasn't among them, I told myself. The idea of letting him cast laughably simple magic *for* me while I stood uselessly by and did nothing...

The spell clicked into place, sending a tingling thrill through my skin where it touched the handle of the lantern.

There.

I strode forward into the whirling snow before I could lose my self-control entirely.

2

Thick white snowflakes swirled around me, bouncing off my spellcast bubble of protection and forming a shifting veil between me and my companions.

Now that Lord Cosgrave was no longer being confronted with the appalling social awkwardness of my presence, his instructions rang out with the natural confidence of any magician in his own territory. "We'll need to spread out, gentlemen, to cover as much area as possible. The toll station is three miles to the north, and Miss Fennell's party should have set off in the right direction, but the land's rough enough that the ladies could have taken a wrong turn nearly anywhere in this weather. All the fairy passageways should be safely locked up from their end at this time of year, thank Christ, but that won't save our guests from rabbit holes and sprained ankles — or from the cold.

"And this isn't only family we're worrying about now. M'wife has great aspirations for her cousin — we may be speaking of a future member of the Boudiccate, if all goes well! The chit's full to bursting with political potential, apparently. So we'd better not lose her in a simple snowstorm, if we don't want to lose all of our funding in the next round of government votes.

"Grant, strike northwest, would you? There's a good man. Quentin, northeast. And Miss Harwood..." He cleared his throat, his expression mercifully obscured by the veil of falling snow between us. "If you wouldn't mind, it's probably best ... that is, as you've only a magnetic compass to rely on in your search..."

"Of course," I said tightly. "I'll walk directly north." *The safest route ...* and also by far the least likely.

I would only discover the perfectly-politically-minded Miss Fennell if she hadn't taken a single misstep along the way.

Cosgrave's exhale of relief was only just audible over the whooshing of the winter wind between us. "Good-o. If you do come across Miss Fennell and her friends, you know, you needn't worry about trying to alert the rest of us. Just come directly home at once. Best thing for all of you, don't you think?"

I couldn't bring myself to answer in words. Instead, I set forward on my assigned path, glad to let the snow whip into a cold wall between us.

Within five feet, the men's voices behind me had turned into a low, indistinguishable rumble. Within ten, I could hear nothing but the soft, inhuman hiss of snow and wind all around me, and every muscle in my shoulders eased in gratitude at the pure relief of it.

The sky was a mix of pale grey and white. The snow rushed past my bubble of protection, leaving me dry and warm and perfectly, beautifully alone within it.

For the first time in four months, there was no one at all to witness me — or to overhear me, either. I could have screamed or raged or finally wept with full abandon for everything that I had lost through my own recklessness, and everything that would have been so different by now if only...

No. I took deep, steadying breaths and forced all thoughts of *if only* from my mind. I would not allow myself to be that pitiful anymore.

I had given up all of my last, desperate hopes of ever retrieving my magic two long months ago. I might never again recognize myself without my magic ... but there was only one way to survive the bleak, powerless future that lay before me. I had to lock away my simmering fury, grief and fear and think only of what lay around me now, in each instant, without ever letting my mind travel to what might happen next.

So I held my lantern high before me and crossed the bare white landscape with long, ground-eating strides that stretched my skirts with every step. I breathed in deep, and I let myself glory in every hiss of snow against my borrowed boots as I strode further and further from the suffocation of the house party and everything that awaited me there.

I was free for this single, icy interlude, and I would absorb every moment of it as a gift.

The pebbles and crushed shells of the Cosgraves' long front drive crunched beneath the snow at first, but they were soon replaced by the elegant gardens that encircled the house, framed with sculpted knotwork hedges for protection. Snow clung and glittered on the bare brown branches, all carefully maintained in their ancient patterns. This deep in the elven dales, only the most reckless landowner would fail to add such protections to her property, no matter how old and how entrenched the treaties between our twinned nations might be.

Luckily, the fairies had already made their own annual pilgrimage deep underground after Samhain, so there were no dangerous fey lights to glitter and distract me from my path across the countryside, nor mushroom circles to carefully avoid. As for the elves ... well, who ever knew what the elves were doing in their ancient halls within the hills and dales of this county? Nothing that they ever cared to share with humans, that was certain. We paid our tolls to use their land and lived in peace, as we had for centuries. That was all that mattered.

Perhaps there were scholars who could have told me more of the elves' secrets, but I realized now that I had never thought to ask in all my hard-won time at the Great Library of Trinivantium. After all, I'd grown up outside these dales, with nothing in my own daily life down south to pique my curiosity ... and back then, I'd had my own magic to focus on without worrying over theirs. *That*, as far as I was concerned, was ancient history — and it was my brother who was the historian in our family.

As I left the knotwork gardens behind, the landscape ahead turned rough and rocky, and I found myself, for the very first time, rather regretting that lost opportunity for knowledge.

The reality of elves might be lost in the mists of time in my own home county, but here, I could quite easily imagine a pair of elven riders, white and glittering as the snow themselves, emerging from a hidden doorway in any one of the high, sprawling hills that rose around me.

There were no neat, plowed fields in this area; only sheep and cattle roamed the bleak beauty of this land, and they were all safely enclosed for the winter. Lady Cosgrave's tenants themselves were, too, in tightly shuttered cottages scattered here and there along the rocky ground. Lights glowed through the thick cloths that covered the windows, but not a single curtain twitched to mark my passage.

It all felt astonishingly freeing. I found myself swinging the lantern in my hand as I walked up the rocky hills, crunching my way through the thin layer of snow and humming a scandalously bawdy old magicians' ballad — one that I had never been meant to learn from my fellow students at the Library when I'd finally, reluctantly been admitted to their company.

I had learnt it, though, of course, absorbing that knowledge with the same greedy joy as the spellwork that I'd fought so hard to master. I still remembered the night I'd first heard it — in Trinivantium's local coffeehouse, which we'd all tumbled into for the evening, collectively tipsy with jubilation from leftover magical residue and the exhilaration of a challenging project well-mastered. As we all found our places along the two long, battered tables in the dark, crowded room, my black academic robes covered every inch of my gown every bit as neatly as the others' robes covered their own trousers and coats; and I think several of them had nearly forgotten by then, after all the initial noise and drama of my arrival, that I wasn't one of their gender as well as their colleague.

It was by far the best evening I had ever had in my life. Free of all chaperones and disapproving tutors, we all sang together late into the night and sent spells crackling with sparkling showers of light over our heads. And then...

When the coffeehouse owner finally, pointedly began to extinguish the candles around us, well after midnight, Rajaram Wrexham had detached his long, lanky figure from the opposite wall, where he'd spent all evening absorbed in conversation with the other scholarship students —

— or at least, he had *seemed* to be utterly absorbed, every time I'd sneaked a secret glance in his direction —

— and walked with unmistakable purpose straight to me.

"We'd better escort each other home, don't you think, Harwood? The streets are dark this late at night."

"You think I can't protect myself?" I demanded.

His dark eyebrows shot up in response. "Hardly. I've seen you at work, remember?"

Aha. A *delicious frisson of satisfaction ran through me as I met his intent gaze and finally realized:* he *had been watching* me, *too...*

Crack!

The unmistakable sound of a branch snapping came from directly behind me, startling me out of my reverie. My heart juddered uncomfortably in my chest as I scanned the rocky hillside around me through the shimmer of falling snow, taking in my surroundings for the first time in far too long.

There were no trees on this barren spot of land. So where had that snapping branch come from?

The last ones I remembered passing had been... *Oh.*

I turned with mingled dread and anticipation, already knowing, somehow, what I would see.

Wrexham stood three feet behind me.

❧

MY EX-FIANCÉ'S TANGLED BLACK HAIR SHOWED THE DISORDER of his spellcast travel; the branch that lay before him must have snapped off one of Lady Cosgrave's elaborate knotwork hedges, caught up in the whirlwind of his passage.

The contrast between the vivid memories that I'd only

just escaped and the reality of his presence before me now was so striking that for a moment I couldn't speak. For one dizzying instant, the two figures — Wrexham then and now — seemed to overlap each other in my vision.

Of course he wasn't that lanky twenty-year-old boy anymore, the intense scholarship student from a Maratha-Anglish sailor's family, with too-long hair, secondhand robes, and the most brilliant magical mind in our class ... at least, until I'd joined mid-year and become his competition.

First, we'd competed for top honors. Then we'd egged each other on. And then...

He had grown into himself over the years, his lankiness filling out into a hard, lean strength. And his work for the Boudiccate had brought him honors far beyond any that we'd ever competed for in our years at the Library, along with comfortable financial security. The gleaming polish on his knee-high boots, and the elegant, multi-caped greatcoat he wore now, were both unmistakable reminders, snapping me out of my daze:

The man I looked at now wasn't the boy who'd once dazzled me. No, he was the adult I'd shouted my most venomous words at two months earlier, when he'd arrogantly and unforgivably refused to understand what should have been obvious for any simpleton to see.

He was the one I'd driven away to save us both.

There were shadows under his eyes now that I hadn't seen two months ago. His light brown cheeks, still dusted with dark stubble from his journey, looked disconcertingly hollow.

But I would not worry about him. I would *not*.

Instead I looked pointedly from his tangled hair to the branch that lay at his feet. "You were in too much of a hurry to protect Lady Cosgrave's hedges? Not very well-mannered for a houseguest."

He arched one dark eyebrow, his narrow lips quirking into a half-smile. "And *you're* worrying about propriety now? You really have changed, Harwood."

The familiar name ran like a knife beneath my ribs, making me suck in a breath. "*Miss* Harwood," I said icily, "if we're worrying about propriety. We're no longer affianced, if you recall."

"Oddly enough," said Wrexham, "I have no difficulty at all in remembering that small detail." He nudged the branch with the toe of one gleaming boot. "You needn't fear that Lady Cosgrave will kick up a fuss. She was the one who urged me to catch you up 'with all haste.' She was concerned about your welfare, apparently." There was a decidedly sardonic tone to his last words.

I could have hissed with exasperation. Curse our hostess! Once a politician, always a practiced maneuverer of people — and of course, she was one of Amy's closest friends. I knew exactly what she'd been up to with that humiliating strategy.

Letting out my held breath, I crossed my arms and glared up at him. "And you? You thought you had to come running to...what? Save me from the terrible dangers of a snowstorm?"

"Hardly," Wrexham said. His smile reappeared, turned rueful. "I've seen you at work, remember?"

Damnation. The echo of our past was too much for me to bear. I turned and struck out blindly across the uneven ground, only hoping that my feet were still carrying me north. "You can tell our hostess that you've confirmed my safety," I called back to him. "So you've done your duty as a guest."

"Ah, but we haven't found Miss Fennell yet, have we?" Wrexham fell smoothly into step beside me, his greatcoat swishing about his long legs. "Lady Cosgrave wishes all the magicians of our party to join the search."

"Then —" *No.* I snapped my teeth shut just in time, before I could give in to temptation and order him to search elsewhere.

My ex-fiancé might be infuriating, but he was no fool. I couldn't afford to drop such obvious clues ... and if I truly hadn't any feelings left for him anymore, as I'd claimed so vehemently two months ago, then I shouldn't mind where he chose to conduct his search. No, I should be perfectly cool and collected in his company.

I said, with poisonous sweetness, "Shall we talk about the weather?"

"If you like." He glanced up at the snow-clouded sky, walking as easily up the steep slope of the hill as if we were taking a morning stroll about a garden. "It wasn't meant to snow for at least another three days. Don't you find this storm a bit peculiar?"

I rolled my eyes. "As if weather wizardry were ever reliable." It was one of the first things we'd been taught after my arrival at the Library, as our tutors fought valiantly to clear our minds of superstition and instill a more Enlightened approach to magic.

"It could be, though. If they forgot about trying to mimic the ancient druids and took a more modern approach — or if someone would finally devote the time and effort to persuading any of the non-human beings to share their own strategies ... hmm." Wrexham broke off, his voice sharpening. "Where are we, exactly?"

"You don't know?" I slanted a glance up at him through

the falling snow. "You just traveled directly here, remember?"

"Yes, but I wasn't aiming for any particular geographical point." His words sounded abstracted as he peered into the distance, frowning. "I was aiming for you, of course."

But there was no *of course* about the matter. That particular spell took an enormous amount of power and effort ... and, far more unsettlingly, a bone-deep familiarity with its target.

I kept my tone light even as my fingers tightened around my lantern and compass. "It's a pity no one in our party knows Miss Fennell well enough to do the same. But — *ahh!*" I gasped as the ground suddenly lurched beneath our feet, sending me stumbling forward. "What was that?"

Beneath us, the ground had re-settled ... but in the distance, a boulder shifted up and down.

Boulders didn't move on their own.

Wrexham and I both turned with the swift, unspoken instinct of long practice until our backs nearly touched and we could survey the entire landscape together.

Snow flurried past my bubble of protection. A rock rolled slowly past my feet, tumbling downhill.

Wrexham said, his voice deceptively casual, "Neither of us knows this territory. So how did you happen to choose your path?"

I grimaced, glad that he couldn't see my face as I made my confession. "Without any finesse whatsoever, I'm afraid. All I have is a plain magnetic compass, so I've followed it."

And I had, even as my wayward memories had wandered elsewhere. My booted feet had walked north across snow-covered fields and even up this rugged hillside, following the compass's magnetic lead...

...But the rest of me hadn't paid nearly enough attention to where I was going.

This was the problem with memories — and with useless, distracting emotions in general. This was why I should have known better than to come to this house party in the first place! I might already have lost my magical abilities, but there was no excuse for giving up my mental capacities as well.

My gaze swept across the barren, rocky hillside that we stood on, identical to every other hill ranging in the distance...until it moved.

Again.

The ground shivered beneath my feet.

Another rock rolled past us.

I took a deep breath and gripped the lantern's handle to hold it steady as the pieces of the puzzle clicked into place. "It seems," I said to my ex-fiancé in as calm a tone as I could muster, "you may have a chance to discuss non-human methods of weather prediction after all ... because I'm reasonably certain that we are standing on a troll."

3

Giant boulders flexed at the edges of what I'd taken to be the hillside as the crouching troll rolled out its massive, grass-covered shoulders, sending the ground shivering and rolling beneath my feet.

It was clearly preparing itself to stand ... at which point we would be tossed willy-nilly off its back.

Frustration rose like acid through my throat as I planted my boots more firmly on the swaying, rocky slope and sought for any viable alternatives. Amy would never forgive me if my carelessness got me killed today after all the work she'd put into keeping me alive and sane over the last four months.

I'd been jesting, of course, about the prospect of conversation with the creature. I had *never* heard of a troll speaking to a human — not even when scooping up untaxed carriages from the road. They communicated with their elven masters, one presumed, but with no one else as far as I knew. The humans who shared these dales with them simply relied on the rules of our ancient treaty for their good behavior ... and on magicians if ever that went wrong.

Of all the times *not* to be able to cast any spells...

"We're too high up to reach the ground in time." I spoke through my teeth.

"It must have been asleep till now — for years, even, to settle so firmly into the ground." Behind me, Wrexham's voice sounded more speculative than worried. "Who knows how long it's been resting here?"

"Until we woke it." I drew a deep breath, trying to force myself into the same analytical mode, as if this were only one of the more challenging magical puzzles that we'd been set at the Library. "It's so much larger than the ones that guard the toll roads."

"Perhaps it's older than they are, too. Or..." Wrexham broke off as the ground shifted again beneath our feet. This time, even more unsettlingly, it began to rise through the air, lifting us higher and higher above the ground as the troll's massive, bent legs slowly began to straighten beneath us. I staggered, and Wrexham's voice sharpened as he dropped down to a wary crouch. "Take my hand, Harwood. It's time for us to leave."

"No." I glowered through the falling snow as I fell to my knees and grabbed hold of a nearby rocky outcropping for balance. I clung onto it, breathing hard, as the ground slanted beneath me. "You cast a travel spell for yourself scarcely ten minutes ago. You can't carry a passenger with you on a second journey now. Not this soon. You'd risk injuring yourself forever." *As I had.*

I would *not* be the means of breaking him, too.

Unfortunately, I couldn't see many other options. By law, we were only allowed to attack the elves' creatures in cases of clear self-defense, not mere *anticipation* of accidental injury. Any magic that Wrexham worked against the troll before it deliberately tried to hurt us — even a simple binding spell to cast it back to sleep — would break those ancient treaty rules in the most disastrous manner.

The Boudiccate would never forgive him for it. Nor would the rest of the nation if the elves were to set the rest of their pet trolls rampaging in revenge.

"*Go*," I said tightly, my fingers clenched around my rocky anchor as we rose higher and higher into the air. "Get yourself to safety, now. I'm the one who made the foolish mistake of walking up here in the first place. I'll find my own way down." *Somehow.*

I couldn't whisk myself to the ground with any spell of my own, nor protect myself from the troll if it chose to lash out at me in its dozy, half-asleep state.

But there had to be something I could still do. There *had* to be. If I didn't believe it was impossible...

What did *impossible* really mean, anyway?

It had been common knowledge all throughout my childhood that a young lady could never be accepted at the Great Library, any more than a human could ever converse with a troll. But that hadn't stopped me, had it?

"Harwood, don't be a fool," Wrexham muttered as I lunged upward. "Take my — damn it, *Harwood!*"

I was already scrambling out of his reach, the force of my frustration propelling me as fiercely across the troll's slanted, rising back as any of the unstoppable metal steam trains that thundered through the southern counties. "*Gothan dag*!" I bellowed, cupping one hand to my mouth as I clung with my other hand to the sloping ground.

It was the language of the old Deniscan invaders who'd carried the trolls with them in the first place over a thousand years ago. Even in the northernmost points of Angland, it had been centuries since almost anyone had spoken it apart from two or three of the most obsessively dedicated historians...

...Including my older brother, as it happened. Jonathan had taught himself as a youth out of academic curiosity, and then taught it to me as a useful secret language. All through my childhood, it had filled our letters to each other and our most private conversations. We'd retreated into it whenever we most needed a safe harbor from our parents' disapproval or his classmates' prying eyes.

Apparently, some creatures in this land were old enough to recognize it too.

The rocky surface beneath us went abruptly still.

Wrexham's dark eyes widened. "You've certainly got its attention," he murmured. He rose to his feet, giving the unmoving landscape a wary look, but he showed no signs of leaving to save himself ... as usual. Would the man *ever* learn the value of a strategic retreat in any area of his life?

But there was no time to waste in that old battle.

"We apologize for disturbing you!" I shouted instead in Densk, aiming my words in the direction of the troll's still-hidden head. "If you could let us safely off your back, please, we would be extremely grateful. And we'd make certain that no one else disturbs your rest any time soon, I promise! We would protect you from any other intruders!"

It was, of course, a perfectly safe promise to make. Once the tenants around here were alerted to the real nature of this "hill," I was more than certain that they would all steer a wide berth around it. If any more incentive was required, Lord Cosgrave could be called in to add magical protections.

But for all the good sense of my strategy, Wrexham was staring at me with open shock.

"Good God," he said. "The tone of your voice... You actually listened to some of your mother's political lessons after all! I've never heard you actually *negotiate* with anyone before. I didn't even know that you could!"

"Pah." I narrowed my eyes at him. Of all the times to ramble nonsense! I had *negotiated* for years to make my entry into the Great Library ... by utterly refusing to give up on my great plans until the world around me finally saw sense and accepted them.

But before I could come up with a properly sizzling retort, the ground suddenly dropped away beneath my feet.

The lantern slipped out of my hand as I fell. I lurched forward just in time to snatch the iron casing from mid-air ... but with both hands full, I landed hard on the troll's rocky back at a distressing angle.

My heart thudded in my tight chest, and my breath came in shallow pants. The spellcast bubble of warmth around me stopped the snow from soaking my coat and gown, but it couldn't stop my knees and elbows from bruising badly. I bit back a curse as I pushed myself upright, only slightly mollified to see that Wrexham, too, had fallen into an undignified pose.

"It appears," I said breathlessly, "that my negotiations may have worked. So —"

The troll's stony knees hit the ground below us with a thud that rocked through my bones and sent us both sprawling in the snow.

"Ouch." Wrexham picked himself up, wincing. "I should have known that if you ever did agree to negotiate on anything, the result would inevitably be painful for both of us."

"Ohhh —!" Growling, I lunged to my feet and shoved the compass into the pocket of my greatcoat. "For once in your life, would you stop talking and *run*?"

I didn't wait to hear his answer. Holding my too-constricting skirts high with my free hand, I leapt, skidded and half-slid down the rocky slope, grateful for Lady Cosgrave's sturdy boots. The lantern's light rocketed around me wildly as it swung from my right hand, sending beams of light shooting through the thickening veil of snow.

The sky above was growing noticeably darker already, shifting from light to dark gray as the pale winter sun slid down toward the horizon. This far north, it would be night-black soon, even though it wasn't yet evening. And then...

Panting, I hurtled down the final yards of the troll's bent back. The creature's earlier movement had dislodged all of the accumulated earth and sod of centuries that had smoothed out the cracks between its crouching limbs when I'd first climbed up it. Now I had to grit my teeth, toss the lantern aside, and take a flying leap across the last ten feet to solid ground, bending my legs and wrapping my arms around my head for self-protection.

Distantly, I heard the sound of glass shattering as I landed and rolled across the snow.

Ow. Ow, ow, ow...

I rolled to a stop, breathing hard.

My shoulder hurt. My ribs hurt. My chest hurt.

It was *glorious.* I felt tinglingly, wildly alive for the first time in ages.

It was the absolute polar opposite of the last four months of smothering safety and silent tears and cosseting, overwhelming solicitude all around me.

Better yet, I had saved us both — with *no* magic required!

Exhilaration flooded my bruised body as I pushed myself to my feet, ignoring all of my aches and twinges along the way. "Well, then!" I smiled sunnily at my ex-fiancé, who stood three feet away from me, carefully brushing down his elegant greatcoat. "Now that I've solved that little problem, we can leave our friend to sleep for another century or two, and..."

A sound like thunder rumbled ominously nearby.

Snow continued to fall around us, soft-looking, white and steady without any hint of rain in sight. Wrexham's head jerked up as I fell silent.

Both of us turned in the same moment to face the crouching troll. I took one nervous step backward.

It wasn't far enough.

The thunder built into a deafening roar as the troll surged upright in one explosive movement that sent rubble and boulders flying through the air. I turned to run, already knowing it was too late.

Before I could take a single step, Wrexham knocked me to the ground, his voice snapping out as his arms wrapped around me. His words were lost in the roar of sound that surrounded us, but the effect was impossible to miss, even with my view half-blocked by his shoulder.

The boulder that had been aiming straight in my direction hung in mid-air for one paralyzed moment before dropping harmlessly to the ground. More and more rubble hit the same invisible wall before giving up and raining onto the ground before us.

I said, my voice reasonably steady given the circumstances, "*That* was a rather more powerful protection spell than Lord Cosgrave set on me earlier."

"A sign that he hasn't spent nearly enough time with you, clearly." Wrexham levered himself up onto his elbows, craning his head to peer up through the flying clouds of rubble. "I don't believe your friend up there is actually trying to attack us at the moment, just shake itself free. Unfortunately, I didn't think to make my protection spell portable, so we'll have to remain here for the duration."

"Hmm." It might be reasonable to grant even the most accomplished magician the benefit of the doubt when he'd been forced to cast a spell at a moment's notice, in the midst of deadly peril. And yet...

I gave my ex-fiancé a suspicious look. Now that the immediate peril had passed, I could finally take note of our position ... and with his arms braced on either side of my head, he covered me entirely, radiating warmth through his greatcoat in the most distracting manner.

I *had* thought, once upon a time, that we fitted together perfectly. But I had never before had the chance to test that theory quite so literally.

What nonsense. I shifted beneath him, trying to ease the disconcerting tingling sensations that were suddenly running through me.

Unfortunately, that movement only made them more intense. My breath was coming more quickly than before. I moistened my lips and fixed my gaze on the underside of his stubborn chin, just above me, to distract myself from other, more dangerous regions nearby.

Most of his throat, of course, was covered by his cravat, but the bits of light brown skin that were exposed looked perilously soft and touchable — almost as soft as the tips of glossy black hair that curled against the thick collar of his coat. If I lifted one hand...

No. I squeezed my eyes shut, forcing my recalcitrant body into submission. The time for allowing myself to be distracted by Wrexham's physical presence was long past. I had not only given up that dream, I had thrown it away with both hands, and with the most vicious repudiation I could manage. If he realized how I was reacting to him now, after all that had passed between us, I would be humiliated forever.

And *that* realization was enough to make me stiffen like a board. My eyes snapped open. "I would have thought," I said sharply, "that all those years of working for the Boudiccate would have given you the ability to calculate the details of your spells more precisely."

"Oddly enough," said Wrexham, still gazing upwards, "in all those years, I've never before been in a situation where you were about to be killed in front of me ... at least not when I could actually prevent it." For a moment, his voice flattened.

I went still, remembering it too. He had been the one who'd found me four months ago, stepping into my workroom barely a moment too late, just as the spell caught me in its grip...

But then he shook his head, and his lips twisted into a rueful grin as he finally looked down at me, his gaze alarmingly focused and intent. "Although ... if I'd ever hoped for a single moment when you were forced to stop running and actually listen —"

"Oh, I think not," I said, and twisted out from underneath him. "The rubble's stopped falling," I told him as I pushed myself swiftly to my feet, breaking through the bubble of his protective spell. "So it's perfectly safe to start moving again."

Wrexham muttered something under his breath. But I chose not to try to decipher his words as I took three perfectly calm and composed — and rapid — steps away from his prone figure.

There. Now I could breathe again. More than that, I could think.

The troll was looming over us, vast and rocky and

unmoving, with its heavy stone arms hanging at its sides. I tipped my head back to peer up at it through the veil of snow and found it gazing down at me.

Its massive mouth opened. A gravelly, throaty roar emerged, as deep as thunder but a hundred times louder.

!!!

Pain battered my head and the earth shook beneath my feet as the troll's roar echoed around the hills. I threw out my arms for balance, fighting to stay upright within that wall of nearly impenetrable noise...

But in the midst of it all, I could just make out a set of words I recognized in the rolling Densk that my brother had taught me so many years ago:

"Meddlers... Hurting... Changing..."

Oh, damnation. "I'm sorry!" I shouted back, cupping my hands around my mouth. "We didn't mean to hurt you —"

But a high, clear voice spoke behind me in Anglish before I could finish bellowing my sentence.

"Oh, he wasn't speaking about the two of *you.*"

I spun around as Wrexham leapt to his feet, his greatcoat billowing around him.

A tall, pale man with hair like glittering shards of ice and a shimmering blue, ankle-length coat stood on the snowy ground just behind me. Every silvery detail of his embroidered coat was bright and clear as a warning to my gaze, for the snowflakes that should have formed a veil between us shot away in all directions instead, clearing a path before him as if in honor ... or in a frenzy to escape.

Not a man. I sucked in a breath as I met his gleaming white gaze through the clear air and realized who — and what — I must be looking at.

The troll wasn't the only ancient creature in the elven dales to have woken to our presence today.

"He was speaking," said the elf lord disdainfully, "of the mischief-makers who've brought this storm down on all of our heads with their thoughtlessness." He arched one narrow, bluish-white eyebrow as he surveyed me. "But I do look forward to watching you keep your binding promise to my pet by dealing with them for him ... *now,* if you please."

4

Without so much as a word or a look exchanged between us, Wrexham and I were suddenly side by side, the thick sleeves of our greatcoats brushing against each other as we jointly faced my accuser. The massive troll loomed behind us, and my head still ached with the grinding echoes of its roar, but there was no question of which danger was more urgent.

Neither of us would dare turn our back on the troll's master.

I wished now that I hadn't released my lantern, shattered though its glass sides might be. Flung in his icily carven face, the iron frame might have won us a moment's grace just when we most needed it to escape. But it lay useless in the snow ten feet away ... and picking it up again now, in the elf lord's presence, could be construed as nothing but an intention to attack.

He smiled unpleasantly as he looked us up and down. "Well? Not so quick to make any promises now, are you? I believe you'll find your earlier promise binding, though, under the terms of our nations' treaty. And those who rashly break their bargains with the elves —"

"No one has broken anything," said Wrexham. His voice was calm, but a thread of steel ran through it. "I am an officer of the Boudiccate, and if a crime has been committed here —"

"*If*?" The elf lord gestured sweepingly, and the snowflakes scurried to get out of his arm's way. "This storm is no act of nature. Someone has been meddling with the land's own magic, and we will all feel the damage soon enough."

"And you simply assume it was a human who did it?" I demanded. The injustice of that, at least, was enough to break the eerie spell of his presence. "How do you know it wasn't one of your own people?"

His upper lip curled. "The laws in our kingdom utterly prohibit any such atrocity of nature, which torments our pets and endangers our hunts to the damage of all. It is our kingdom, not your nation, which is most harmed by this unnatural storm. Any observer with a shred of logic would tell you that one of your own mages — always so prone to risks and wild experimentation — must be the ones directing all of it. Your current mishmash of various tribes may claim to restrict their experiments, but when you leave a squabbling group of human women in control..." His eyes narrowed with sudden, dangerous interest, and his voice dropped as he stepped closer to me.

An icy chill pierced the bubble of my spellcast warmth, making me shiver.

"Take yourself as an example, woman," he murmured, his white eyes fixed on mine. "There's the scent of magic running through your bones, though your people claim to restrict its use to men. How ... *very* ... interesting. You, too, have been meddling where you don't belong, haven't you?"

I stiffened, fury simmering in my blood, but Wrexham spoke first. "Careful," he said softly. "Your king may choose to treat his own nation's ladies with disdain, but ours has been governed well by them for centuries. You would not wish to offend the Boudiccate."

"Indeed, I can see just how frightening a force they must be, when their rules can be broken with such impunity." The elf lord laughed, a jingle of broken bells. "And those who call themselves *men* but choose to submit themselves to such rulers ... but then, I'm not looking at a born lord, am I?" He flicked Wrexham with a dismissive glance. "You're one of the Boudiccate's vagabond upstarts, aren't you? Promoted far beyond your station, with no real understanding of your betters ..."

If he couldn't see Wrexham's strength, he was a fool, and there was no point in taking offense at any of his jibes. I drew a deep breath and spoke with forced composure, drawing on the memory of my mother's old political negotiations. I'd been forced to observe them only too often as her unwilling apprentice in the years before she'd finally given up on me. "Our weather wizards can barely predict whether it will snow or rain with any accuracy," I told him, refusing to lower my gaze as I spoke the humiliating truth. "You must know we haven't any magicians who could manage the weather itself and summon a storm like this one."

The elf lord's smile could have cut through frost. "Oh, I don't believe for an instant that any of you could ever *manage* it. No, I think you were — as usual — playing with forces you couldn't possibly hope to control."

The accusation struck hard and close to home. My throat clenched. For a moment I couldn't speak.

"You should have known you could never manage it..."

Wrexham's shouted words from months ago hung in the air like frozen breath.

I did not turn to meet his gaze when I felt him glance at me. I couldn't — not if I wished to control my expression in front of our common enemy.

But I felt a core of unbreakable ice building up inside me, shoving aside the softer, warmer — *weaker* — feelings that had been creeping furtively back into their old familiar places in the last half hour of forced proximity.

I would not make myself so vulnerable again.

"*If* it was a human," I told the elf lord, ice coating my words, "then we will find him. You may depend upon it."

Wrexham stirred beside me. "Harwood —"

"Fine," I snapped, without sparing him a glance. "*I'll* find him myself, then. I was the one to make the binding promise. I should be the one to fulfill it."

"Indeed you must," said the elf lord, "or pay the price. And the promise that you made, as I recall, was hardly so narrow-minded as only to protect my pet *if* the malefactor happened to be human."

I frowned. "But —"

"You can't be serious!" Wrexham's voice was a near-snarl, his shoulders hunching as if he were having to force himself to stay in place. "You know none of us are allowed into your private halls. How can you possibly expect her to hunt for a criminal there?"

"Oh, I certainly don't." The elf-lord laughed. "But then, I never forced her to make that foolish promise, did I?"

In that moment, he was every man who had ever laughed out loud in disbelief when he'd heard that I wished to learn magic and every woman who had ever raised her eyebrows in pity ... or whispered afterward, when she'd thought I couldn't hear, that she'd *always known this would come of it in the end*. The blood was thundering in my ears as I glared at him, and the snow swirled wildly around us, as if it could sense the raw disorder in my chest, where every one of my scabbed wounds had been torn wide open and exposed to the pitiless cold air.

"*I will keep my promise*," I told him, enunciating every word with precision.

The elf lord tipped his head to the side, as if preparing another verbal stab.

Wrexham spoke first, though, his voice so steady that anyone who didn't know him well might have missed the thread of deadly fury running underneath his words. "She has another promise that needs keeping first. We've been sent out to search for a lost party of guests. Before any of us can begin another mission —"

"Oh, *them*?" The elf lord shook his head sadly. "Poor little lost lambs. You people are careless, aren't you? Do you know they weren't even carrying any iron with them on their journey?" His glance shifted and lingered for one, visibly amused moment on the frame of my broken lantern, lying uselessly on the ground nearby.

Sudden panic gripped me as I followed his gaze. Horror stories were still passed down, after all these centuries, about the vicious games that the elves had once loved to play with unprotected humans, before the last, most devastating war had finally bought us the hard-won treaty between our nations. The elves wouldn't dare break that treaty now, after so long — would they?

But if Miss Fennell's party had broken one of the treaty's more obscure rules in some way, without realizing...

I didn't need to understand the finer details of elven politics to know, without a fraction of a doubt, that the elf lord in front of me would leap at the opportunity for punishment.

"What have you done to them?" I breathed.

Every inch of my body ached to cast a spell that would banish the smugness from his face. But it would be a Pyrrhic victory indeed that left me lying broken in the snow — and at his mercy — afterward.

"I?" The elf lord raised both eyebrows in haughty reproach. "Why, I couldn't lay a finger on *them*, under the terms of our agreement. Our noble king would never hear of such a thing." His lips twisted into a sneer. "Wasn't it fortunate, then, that I found *you,* little meddler, as a reward for my good behavior?"

I sucked in a breath. Wrexham started forward.

The elf lord lifted one hand and clicked his fingers.

The spellcast bubble around me burst, and snow hurled itself against me, flinging wet, choking handfuls of flakes into my face until I had to bend over, gagging and coughing, covering my nose and my mouth with my hands. My ears were half-covered by my hood, but it wasn't enough as the snow and wind buffeted me. It wasn't nearly enough. And then...

I could just make out the muffled sound of Wrexham's voice somewhere in the distance, loud and agitated. But in my head, a slithering, unwelcome invasion, I could suddenly hear the elf lord's own piercing whisper:

"You have one se'ennight from the completion of your first mission to keep your promise to my pet, little meddler. But when you fail, I'll be waiting here to exact your payment — and this time, no one from my nation or yours will be able to deny me. Oh, I've been waiting such a long time to play my favorite games again."

The snow and wind abruptly fell away from me. In the

sudden, deafening silence inside my own head, my breath came in heavy pants. Every bruise on my body ached. Slowly, painfully, I straightened, blinking the leftover wet, stinging snowflakes out of my eyes.

The elf lord was gone. My spellcast bubble was back. And Wrexham was staring at me from a few feet away, his dark eyes wide with what looked like surprise.

Or rather... *Wait*. His gaze was fixed beyond me. At...

I twisted, uncomfortably, to look over my own shoulder.

"Oh, I say!" The tallest of the four young women who stood clustered behind me in a rather damp-looking but festive group laughed with delight and pointed up at the troll, who stood massive and unmoving against the darkening sky. "*He*'s quite a big brute, isn't he? I shouldn't care to run afoul of *him!*"

I sighed, shoulders sagging, as I took in the elf lord's parting gift. "Miss Fennell, I presume."

Wrexham had, after all, told the elf lord that I couldn't begin my next mission before my last one was complete ... so the elf lord had completed it for me.

How terribly, terribly helpful of him.

Miss Fennell grinned as she took us in. "Come to rescue us, have you? Sent by my cousin, I assume? Very decent of you, really!"

"Indeed," I said sourly, trying not to take in Wrexham's expression. "Your cousin was worried about you."

...And an hour earlier, I would have deeply relished the idea of being the one to find Lady Cosgrave's missing cousin, without using any magic along the way.

Somehow, though, in the wake of the elf lord's visit, it didn't feel like quite the victory I'd hoped for after all.

❦

THERE WAS NO OUT-STRIDING MISS FENNELL AND HER friends. Young, rowdy, cheerful, slightly tipsy, and all of them apparently untouched by their experience, they surrounded us in a laughing, jostling group that — all too soon — resulted in the inevitable idea of a jolly sing-song to speed our way home.

I tried to speed my own footsteps, but it was no use. Miss Fennell looped one arm through mine and matched me step for step, heavy traveling skirts swishing about her boots, while she sang at the top of her impressively strong lungs. Wrexham had done her and her friends the basic courtesy of spelling them safety from the elements as well, so even my secret fantasy of snow falling into her open mouth was thwarted.

...Not that she could truly be considered to blame for *all* of this afternoon's mishaps, I admitted sourly to myself as we marched across the snowy landscape, our party's merry yodeling echoing loudly around the hills.

Still, so much youthful exuberance was difficult to bear with an aching body and an uncomfortable new set of regrets.

I wasn't looking forward to admitting to Amy all that had occurred out here this afternoon. Worse yet, I could tell that Wrexham was only waiting to give me his own opinion on the matter.

That, at least, I could prevent. As he edged closer through the crowd of cheerful travelers, his dark brows bent forbiddingly, I jerked Miss Fennell forward and grasped the arm of her closest friend — one Miss Banks — with my free hand.

"There!" I said brightly. "Now we're joined in a chain!"

"Ha! Delightful." Miss Fennell beamed.

Her friend, a slighter girl with pale skin flushed pink

with either excitement or alcohol, and what looked like fine blonde hair beneath her hood, smiled shyly at me from our newly intimate vantage point ... and then her eyes widened in sudden recognition.

"Oh. Oh! Are you —? That is..."

Oh no. I felt Wrexham's wry gaze on the back of my neck as he dropped back to wait just behind me.

There would be no escape if I released her arm now. But even my lack of answer had been too much of a hint, apparently.

"You *are* Cassandra Harwood, aren't you?" she breathed. "Oh, I knew it! I've been so hoping to meet you. I have *so many* questions I've been dying to ask you, all about what happened to you this summer!"

Oh, damnation.

Cursing my life, my ex-fiancé and myself in equal measure, I smiled ferociously at my young interrogator and kept her arm tightly trapped in mine. "Of course," I said. "But not right now. It's time to sing!"

And with my ex-fiancé following every step, I sang furiously all the way to Cosgrave Manor.

✤ 5 ✤

In the flurry of greetings that met us at the door, I was finally able to detach myself from young Miss Banks, using the pretext of disposing of my outerwear. A quick duck and a dive behind the group of gathered visitors all exclaiming and commenting upon our arrival, a careful swerve past the servants hovering behind them, and I was free of my would-be questioner...

...But my ex-fiancé fell smoothly into step beside me. "May I take your coat?" he inquired sardonically.

"Certainly," I told him, and tossed Jonathan's greatcoat straight at his chest. Then I spun away on one heel of Lady Cosgrave's excellent boots and strode across the blue-and-gold-tiled floor of the entry hall as quickly as I could.

With his annoyingly long legs, Wrexham had no difficulty keeping up, but at least he couldn't grasp my elbow to stop me with both of his arms full of thickly piled coat. "Harwood —!" he began, in a near-snarl.

"Ah, *there* you are!" Someone far more frightening stood before us: my sweet, smiling sister-in-law, waiting for me in the open archway between me and the rest of the house.

Her bright gaze moved from me to my ex-fiancé. Her eyebrows rose. Her mouth dropped open to form an "O" of delight that filled me with instant and overwhelming dread.

"*No!*" I said hastily. "No, we haven't reconciled. And we're certainly not going to! In point of fact, I can't even speak to anyone at all anymore. I'm — I'm terribly, terribly tired. From my exertions. I think I need a nap."

"Cowardly, Harwood," Wrexham muttered. "An unworthy move."

I winced but stood my ground.

Amy's eyes narrowed as she studied me. "You do look tired," she said. "I'd better show you to your room."

"You needn't —" I began, just as Wrexham said, "Mrs. Harwood, if you please —"

"The servants," she told me firmly, "are all occupied, and you couldn't possibly find it on your own. As for you, Mr. Wrexham..." She gave my ex-fiancé a firm nod. "I'm sure we'll both be delighted to speak with you later."

"Delighted," he said wryly, and bowed deeply before turning away without any further argument.

My mouth dropped open in outrage as I stared after him.

If Wrexham actually possessed the heretofore-unseen ability to recognize an impossible battle when he saw one ... then why had he never been intimidated out of arguing by *me*?

But there was no time to fathom the depths of that injustice as Amy tucked a firm hand into the crook of my arm and swept me, simmering, through the archway. She chatted happily all the way as she led me up a curving set of stairs, the walls beside it lined by stately portraits of the many women who'd proudly led the Cosgrave family and the nation itself through the centuries. Every one of the Ladies

Cosgrave, judging by the weighty gold-and-silver torcs painted around all of their necks, had been a member of the Boudiccate in her own turn ... and it was impossible, as I passed that grand and glowering procession, not to be entirely aware of my own bruised and disordered appearance and generally unwomanly lack of dignity by comparison.

Even my own mother, by the end, had given up on my ever following in her famous path. Still, it had been rather easier to stand strong in that recollection four months earlier, before I'd failed in the vocation for which I'd given up her shining legacy and pride.

"...And of course," Amy continued as she swept me off the staircase and down a branching corridor lit by warm, expensive fey-lights set in spellbound sconces along the wall, "there are all the latest troubles with the elves to complicate matters, and —"

"*What?*" I stopped abruptly, tugging her to a halt along with me.

Amy's eyes widened as she looked at me. "My goodness, Cassandra, I didn't imagine you were actually listening to me. I've never known you to be interested in politics before!"

I forced myself to unclench my jaw and suck in a deep breath. "What were you saying about the elves, exactly?"

"Surely you must have heard — well. No. You haven't been following the news lately, have you?" She looked pained at her own misstep.

I gave her arm a bracing squeeze. "Oh come now, Amy. You know perfectly well I was never a great reader of newspapers even before ... what happened." No, I'd been far too consumed with my own magical pursuits beforehand, and afterward ... well. "You needn't worry about any tender feelings on my part," I said briskly. "Only explain to me what's been happening."

She sighed and tugged me with her along the corridor, leaning into my side and lowering her voice as we walked. "It's more what *hasn't* happened, actually. The elves send a representative each year at the end of Samhain, when the fairies make their great pilgrimage underground. At least one elf always stands beside an officer of the Boudiccate to jointly light the fairies' passage."

"And?" I glanced instinctively at the closest spellbound sconce on the wall nearby. The fey-light there burned golden-bright, illuminating the leaping horse pattern of the mosaic art along the wall in a warm, caressing glow ... but of course that was little rational comfort; it would continue to burn regardless of its creator's fate. Like fey-silk (soft as butterflies' wings, the advertisements always claimed), fey-lights cost the earth, and for good reason. They lasted for years with no need for renewal, even during the darker turnings of the year when the unpredictable fairies themselves were safely contained underground.

"This year, no representative from the elven court arrived." Amy's face tightened, fine white lines of tension showing beneath her warm brown skin. "The elven king sent his regrets instead, and his best wishes."

"And...?" I frowned, thinking of the icy elf-lord I'd just faced. "That sounds like the best possible outcome, *I* should think. If you can keep the elves' friendship without being afflicted with their company —"

"Oh, really, Cassandra!" Amy shook her head at me, unaccustomed exasperation leaking into her voice. "I know you've spent most of your life fighting not to be drawn into politics, but just this once, take a moment to actually *think* about it. They haven't missed that ceremony for four hundred years! It was either a deliberate snub, in which case our treaty is in grave danger — or else a sign that their own court is in such disarray that he didn't trust any one of his courtiers to meet with us in public this year."

"I see." I nibbled at my lower lip. What was it that the elf-lord had said to defend himself against the charge of kidnapping? *"Our noble king would never hear of such a thing."* But his tone...

"So we might have the king's best wishes, but not his nobles'."

"We might," Amy agreed grimly. "In which case, we are in very dangerous waters indeed." My gentle sister-in-law's face was, for once, set in forbidding lines — not the usual warm, loving expression of my affectionate sister-in-all-but-blood, but that of a woman of certain power and intellect ... who should, if luck and justice prevailed, be selected as the newest member of the Boudiccate the very next time an opening arose.

She *should* have been granted my mother's seat, as I myself would have been if matters had gone as planned by the older generation — but there was no time to meditate on that old injustice now as Amy continued:

"Without being allowed entrance to their halls, we can't do any more than guess at what might be happening inside them. But our last ambassador returned to her family at the turning of the summer solstice, and they haven't authorized a new one since."

She stopped at a white-paneled door and turned its bronze handle — shaped as a leaping stag in tribute to the male Cosgraves' own magical contributions to the family history — as she spoke. "Oh, they don't *say* that they've closed their court to us entirely — they couldn't, without breaking the treaty — but they've come up with one excuse after another ever since. One ambassador is too young, another is too old; it's simply impossible to make any decisions until a certain elven courtier returns from his travels..."

She stepped aside, ushering me before her into a warm, white-and-gold room with a canopied bed, a large window facing out onto the snowy darkness, and a giant allegorical painting of Boudicca's victory hanging on the wall over the fireplace.

"But," she finished, closing the door firmly behind her, "they all end with the same result. We have no ambassador in their court; we know something is amiss but don't know what; and poor Lady Cosgrave is preparing to host the winter solstice now with no idea whether our allies will even bother to attend the very ceremony that's meant to seal our alliance for another year."

"Ah." My gaze slipped to the glass window and the darkness beyond, where the elf-lord and his troll both waited ... somewhere. "So." I took a breath. "It's rather important, then, that we not do anything to offend them at this point."

"Cassandra!" Amy let out a startled burst of laughter. "How can you even jest about such a thing? It's no laughing matter!"

"No," I agreed glumly. "I imagine not."

The expressions on the kneeling Roman soldiers' faces, in the nearby painting, echoed my feelings rather well.

"Now." Amy plopped down onto the bed and patted the mattress invitingly. "No more excuses from you, please, darling. What on earth were you and Wrexham up to out there, to send you home in such a state?" Her eyebrows furrowed, her expression becoming fierce. "He wasn't insulting to you, was he?"

"No! Of course not." I stalked over to the window, unable

to hold her gaze. The curtains hadn't been lowered yet; I gripped the window-frame with tight fingers, embracing the damp chill that emanated from the dark glass.

The protection spells scrolled in iron along the edges of this frame wouldn't be enough to protect me if the elf-lord came; the last war we'd fought had been more than proof enough of that. No, these spells would only keep out a minor fairy, at the most ... and even if I still possessed my old powers, I couldn't fight back without sacrificing my nation's safety in exchange.

It was a startlingly bitter gift to discover that I still had more to lose, after all, than I had spent the past two months believing.

But if I told my sister-in-law the truth of the danger I was facing, I might as well rip that treaty up with both hands and damn the safety of the rest of our nation forever ... because Amy never, ever gave up on the people she loved.

No. I'd spent the past four months being cosseted by my family, but this was one problem I would have to face alone.

My reflection was a ghost in the window before me. I said, keeping my tone as idle as possible, "You don't know of any weather wizards in this party, do you?"

"Here?" Amy, bless her, took the change of subject in stride. I saw her eyebrows rise in her reflection, but after only a moment's pause, she said, "I imagine at least half the husbands here must work magic. I know all of the members of the Boudiccate married magicians, certainly. But I've never asked about any of their specialties. That was always..." She stopped abruptly, but I could easily finish her sentence for her:

That was always your business, not mine.

I took one long, steady breath and then another, my

breath frosting the glass in front of me. "Would you find out, please?" I asked. "If you could?"

"Of course." Amy's tone gentled. "But darling..."

My shoulders stiffened. I knew that tone only too well.

"You know what the physicians said," my sister-in-law murmured, with sympathetic pain lining every word. "*Any* use of magic is prohibited. I know that weather wizardry isn't quite the same as the sort you used to work on —"

"Used to *cast*," I gritted through my teeth. "I used to *cast* magic. That's what it's called."

The pity on Amy's reflected face was unbearable. I closed my eyes to shut it out, my fingers tightening around the window-frame.

"I beg your pardon," I said quietly. "I shouldn't have interrupted you so rudely."

Amy sighed. "Never mind." Silk swished behind me, followed by the brush of footsteps on the polished wooden floor. I opened my eyes and found her standing behind me with her folded hands resting on her rounded stomach, gazing gravely at my reflection in the window. "You know we'll always help with anything you ask," she said softly. "And I will ask about any weather wizards who might be here. But please, darling, remember: there is more to you than your magic. There *always* was."

Her words pierced a too-thin shell inside my chest. I let out a half-laugh as pain flooded out through the opening. "Magic wasn't just what I cast, it was what I *was*. You, of all people, should know that! By the time you met me —"

"I *know*," she said firmly. "I know you. And I know how tightly you had to shut out everything else to keep from losing your own purpose and being swept away by your mother's great plans for you instead. But I know something else, too: Wrexham, for one, never wanted you for your magic."

"Oh, Amy." Giving up, I tipped my head forward against the damp, cold glass, letting my eyes fall shut as memories overwhelmed me. "Of course he did," I said in a near-whisper. "If you knew just how strong our castings used to be when we worked together..." It had been a perfect partnership. It had been beyond exhilarating. It had been...

"He would have left you four months ago if that was all he'd cared about," said my sister-in-law flatly.

I pulled myself upright, shaking myself out of the maudlin memories as I gathered my strength and turned to face her. "Wrexham is a good man," I said wearily. "He would never willingly abandon anyone in need, much less someone he'd cared about. And when you add in his sheer, bloody-minded stubbornness..."

"Yes?" Amy raised her eyebrows, looking ironic.

If there was a message in that expression, I had no interest in reading it. Instead, I gritted my teeth and met her gaze full-on. "I have no interest in being Wrexham's pity project," I bit out, "or the burden hanging about his neck. And fortunately, I don't have to resign myself to either fate — because, although you seem to have somehow forgotten this, we are *no longer betrothed*!"

"Hmm." Amy gave me a measuring look. Then, maddeningly, her lips curved into an understanding smile. "You *are* tired," she said. "It wasn't only an excuse after all." Reaching out, she patted my arm consolingly. "I'll see you at suppertime. You'll feel better by then."

Argh! I had to press my lips together to keep my groan of frustration from emerging.

The moment that the door closed behind her, I gave in.

Scooping up a pillow from the bed, I pressed it to my face and let out a safely muffled howl.

There was some satisfaction in letting my feelings out, after all. But it couldn't change the truth.

In only two hours, the supper bell would ring. Wrexham would be waiting. So would Amy ... and so would a whole party full of happy, practicing magicians, laughing and toasting and arguing over spells that I would never, ever be allowed to cast again.

Cowardly though it might be, I wanted to barricade my bedroom door and stay hidden in this room for the next two full weeks of our visit. But...

"You have one se'ennight." The elf-lord's remembered voice whispered in my ear.

I set my teeth and braced myself as I dropped the pillow back onto my bed.

It was time to prepare myself for an evening of social gaiety ... because like it or not, I had a rogue magician to catch and only one week in which to do it.

6

When the supper bell sounded, deep and pure, two hours later, I rose from the edge of my bed where I'd been waiting and walked toward the door with my head held high. *No more hiding*, I told myself firmly.

I had drunk a full pot of hot, fortifying tea. I had spent a satisfying half-hour coming up with my most inventive curses for the situation. And most importantly of all, I had prepared myself for social warfare.

If there was one thing that Angland's greatest politician had successfully taught her recalcitrant daughter, it was the usefulness of a really good set of sartorial armor.

Tonight, I was wearing my finest bronze silk gown with a golden, braided rope belted underneath my bosom and a chain of shining pearls around my neck. A shawl of shimmering fey-silk was draped gracefully around my shoulders, and my long-suffering maid, Aoife, had arranged my hair into a braided crown worthy of Boudicca herself.

I was ready. No matter who or what awaited me outside — whether it was Amy, Wrexham, or the elf lord himself —

I would meet them with calm confidence and sweep unhindered on my way.

I turned the stag-shaped door handle and stepped out onto the carpeted corridor, braced for battle.

It was empty. From the top to bottom of the long hallway, I didn't see a single soul.

My shoulders sagged with relief. Letting out my held breath, I turned left and started at an easy pace for the staircase ... just as the door across from mine flew open.

"Oh!" The voice that spoke behind me was young, female and breathy, and it was all too horribly familiar. "What a surprise! I mean, Miss Harwood, what a marvelous coincidence it is that we both happened to be ready at the exact same moment!"

Oh, for...

It was the most appallingly bad acting that I had ever witnessed. I squeezed my eyes shut in pain as I stopped, forced by courtesy to reply despite myself.

"Miss Banks," I said flatly. "What a marvelous coincidence indeed."

"Isn't it?" Beaming, she swooped in on me, letting her door fall heavily shut behind her. No longer covered by a heavy cloak, her fair hair was curled into fine ringlets about her thin white face, which was gently flushed with excitement. "I was so hoping to find the chance to have another chat with you!"

"Were you?" I asked dryly. "I had no idea."

But it was impossible to escape such a well-planned ambush with mere sarcasm. Smiling hopefully, Miss Banks took her place at my side. "Shall we walk to supper together?"

I hesitated, my gaze searching the corridor with real

hope this time. If only another guest would emerge to join us now...

No such luck. Every door in the corridor remained firmly closed, and the sound of convivial cheer floated up through the floorboards. Apparently, we were the last stragglers. *So be it.*

"How delightful," I said, and strode down the hallway as swiftly as I could.

She hurried to keep up. "I've been longing to speak to you for simply *ages*, Miss Harwood! You have no idea how many questions I want to ask you. How you managed your entry into the Great Library in the first place, and whether it was difficult to be the only lady there, and, if you would — if you *could* explain to me exactly what went wrong, when you lost your powers all those months ago —"

"Miss Banks." I swung around, stopping in my path and baring my teeth in the vicious parody of a smile. "I have *not* lost my powers. I am perfectly capable of casting a spell now with just as great an effect as I could have managed five months ago."

"But..." Her blonde eyebrows drew together. "I thought — that is, everyone said ... you know, everyone has been saying —"

"The *spell* would still work," I said tightly, "but *I* wouldn't." At the sight of her baffled expression, I jerked my shoulders impatiently, trying to loosen the knotted muscles of my back. "Casting any spell, even a small one ... would kill me. Apparently."

"Because — women really aren't suited to magic, after all?" Her brown eyes looked suddenly huge and tragic. "Is that why it happened?"

"No!" I snapped. "Being a woman had nothing to do with it. The same could have happened to any gentleman magician — and it has in the past." Not often, certainly; but it was enough of a risk that our teachers at the Great Library had warned us of the danger of over-extending ourselves in our training, and Jonathan had found mentions of similar incidents all throughout the library's historical records. The effect was rare, but hardly unheard of.

I had still thought, at the time, that it was worth the risk ... but only because I'd never actually believed that any such thing could ever happen to *me.*

The memory of my own reckless folly was unbearable.

I glared at my interrogator, giving up on subtlety. "This," I said, "is a deeply personal line of enquiry, Miss Banks. May I ask why you feel so free to pursue it with a stranger?"

Her fair skin flushed in a wave of red that swept up from her neck to cover her cheeks. Still, she stood her ground and held my gaze. "I have to," she said quietly. "I have no choice, you see. If I can't prove that what happened to you won't happen to me, I'll never be allowed into the Great Library myself."

My eyes widened. We stared at each other for a moment in silence, as my heartbeat suddenly thrummed through my skin and her words echoed through my head.

"I'll never be allowed into the Great Library..."

"You ... want to study magic?" My voice sounded strangely distant in my ears.

She nodded, her thin face pinched with tension. "I must," she said. "I've always yearned to. And now — now, it's the only way. For me *and* for Miss Fennell, both."

What? I shook my head, remembering that jolly, striding creature I'd met earlier. "Miss *Fennell* wants to study magic, too? I thought she was famously politically minded." She'd certainly *seemed* like a young woman destined to run the nation one day, whether the nation happened to care for the experience or not.

"She is," said Miss Banks. "And she'll enter the Boudiccate within the next ten years, I'm certain of it. It's what she's always dreamed of, just as I've always dreamed of magic. But..." She stopped, and drew a breath. "If she wants to be accepted as a member, she has to marry a magician. Lady Cosgrave told her so. Otherwise, she'll be like your sister-in-law — never quite accepted into the inner circle."

"*What*?" I demanded. The sudden influx of information in that brave, wavering voice was overwhelming. "What does Amy have to do with all of this?"

Miss Banks shrugged unhappily. "We've all heard the story. It was Boudicca's second, magician-husband who stood by her side when she led her great rebellion, and helped her expel Rome from our shores forever. Now, each member of the Boudiccate is expected to form that partnership in her own turn."

Whereas Amy ... Amy was already married to Jonathan, my history-loving brother, who had fought just as hard to escape his magical heritage as I had fought to claim it.

How had I never made that connection before?

Of course my mother had never felt required to warn me of that rule. She would have simply assumed that I would marry a magician, as every other woman in our family had for generations. Knowing my own rebellious pull toward magic, she would have considered it a foregone conclusion.

Still, Amy must have known the rule, too — even discussed it with Lady Cosgrave when she was so pointedly passed over for my mother's seat on the Boudiccate. I'd never understood why that snub had occurred ... but then, she would never have told me *or* Jonathan that truth, would she? She would have been far too concerned with saving our feelings even as her own were trampled.

My jaw clenched as fury built inside me. "What utter idiocy," I snarled. "As if there weren't plenty of magicians ready to defend the Boudiccate, without any marriages being involved in the matter."

"Nevertheless, it's still the rule," said Miss Banks quietly. "And that's why I have to study magic, you see. It's the only way that Miss Fennell and I can wed."

Her words lingered for a moment in the nearly-empty hallway before I made any sense of them. Then my eyebrows rose. "Oh," I said. "*Oh.*"

Well, that wasn't unheard of either ... at least not in ordinary society. It was a truth universally acknowledged that women were the more pragmatic sex; that was why we were expected to run the government, while men attended to the more mystical and imaginative realm of magic. So it was commonly accepted that every once in a while, two ladies with no interest in bearing children might well find a more sensible match in each other than in a gentleman.

And yet...

"Would they allow it?" I asked. "I've never heard of a Boudiccate member without a husband." I'd accepted that all my life as mere hidebound tradition, without ever thinking the matter through — but of course, now that Miss Banks had pointed it out, their mimicry of the great Boudicca's own pairing was obvious. *How* had I not solved that mystery myself long ago, to finally understand the reasons behind Amy's snub?

The answer was damnably simple: *Because I wasn't paying enough attention.*

That decision had been made just after my mother's death, when I'd been beset by grief for her loss and for all those bitter battles that we would never have a chance, anymore, to forgive ... but even as I'd wept and raged every night for her cut-short life, I'd spent my days at the Library in a grim blur of unbroken focus, throwing myself into my studies harder than ever before.

Oh, I'd still been outraged for Amy's sake when I'd heard the news, for all that she'd made light of her disappointment in her letters to me...

But when it really came down to it, one truth had dominated: It wasn't magic, so I hadn't been interested enough to pursue the matter any further.

It was an uncomfortable realization to make about myself. More uncomfortable yet was Miss Banks's steady, expectant stare as it rested on my face. "There never was a lady who cast magic, either," she said, "until you."

"Quite." I swallowed hard.

What had I told myself, only minutes earlier? *Time to stop hiding,* indeed.

I'd retreated to the safety of my old bedroom in my family house and locked out every visitor so that I would never have to hear what the world might say of my notorious fall.

But clearly, there were other women who *had* been listening while I'd stayed sheltered with my fingers in my ears.

None of them deserved to be denied their own future for my failures.

A door opened in the corridor behind us. The sound of a tuneless whistle emerged.

I took a deep breath. "I will tell you everything," I promised Miss Banks in a whispered rush. "And I'll do it within a se'ennight." I could put it off no longer. "Will you walk with me in Lord Cosgrave's knot garden one morning after breakfast? We can talk privately then."

"Of course." Her face blazed with such hope, it was painful to look upon.

Had I looked that way, too, when I'd first sensed the doors of the Great Library opening to me?

The whistling behind us broke off. "I say!"

It was my older brother's voice; I turned to find Jonathan smiling affably, his thick brown hair rumpled as if he'd been pulling at it with his fingers and a dab of dark blue ink smeared against his jaw. "I thought *I'd* be the last one to supper," he said. "I'm glad to find you two still here. I had to finish up a rather urgent note I was writing — a bit of an addendum to that article of mine for the *Journal of Deniscan Studies*. I've been reading the proof copies, you see, and they've got the footnotes all wrong!"

"Horrors." I shook my head at him as I reached over to dab away the ink with one finger and Miss Banks watched, eyes wide and curious. "Have you really left poor Amy to escort herself down to supper?"

"Oh, she doesn't mind," Jonathan said blithely. "All the more time to talk politics with her friends, you know, without having to explain the fine details to me as she goes along — and it's not as if I've much of interest to contribute to their husbands' conversations. All that high drama over the proper wording of spells..." He smiled ruefully at me. "Come and help me bear it?"

"Of course." I slipped one arm through his, grateful for his familiar, solid strength and the unspoken support behind it — because for all that he'd phrased it as his own cry for help, he knew perfectly well how much I'd been dreading this first supper in magical company again.

Partners against the world. It was the way we'd always

been, ever since we'd grown old enough to realize that the world — including our own parents — believed that the passions that drove us both had to be stamped out for our own good.

But Amy...

"Amy really is very patient with us, isn't she?" I said thoughtfully.

"She won't be for long, if we miss the start of supper." Jonathan gave my arm an affectionate squeeze. "We'd better hurry."

So we did.

⁂ 7 ⁂

We did not miss the start of supper, although it was a near thing. The doors at the far end of the green salon were just swinging open, and the gathered guests were milling around in preparation to pass through them, when the three of us stepped through the salon entrance. Miss Banks slipped away from my side immediately, seeking — I presumed — Miss Fennell; Jonathan smiled and nodded to the various groups around us, laughing in good-humored acceptance of the jests tossed his way (*"Couldn't pull your nose out of your old scrolls in time, eh, Harwood?"*) and volleying back jests of his own that sent the other men into shouts of laughter; and I rose up onto my tiptoes, as discreetly as possible, to scan the crowd for magical suspects.

I only recognized around half of the gentlemen in the crowd. The older husbands of the Boudiccate, of course, had all been regular guests at my mother's house parties. A few of my own classmates were scattered through the room, too, although none I'd been particularly close to ... and from the way their glances skittered off me, I doubted they would be seeking me out to trade reminiscences during this visit.

I would have to steel myself to approach some of them, though, despite our mutual discomfort. At the very least, they were all sure to have spent more time socializing with other magicians in the field than I had in the last few years, which meant that they'd have far more of an insight into who might be practicing weather wizardry at this party.

That particular specialization might be offered as an option at the Great Library, but not a single student in my year had chosen to pursue it, and for good reason. Weather wizardry was a profitable profession for any magician with limited talent or ambition — after all, every newspaper or almanac-publisher wanted a weather wizard on-staff at all times, and the government, too, was willing to pay ridiculously well for their predictions, no matter how unreliable those predictions might be — but as the disdainful elf-lord had pointed out earlier, our ancient treaties with magical creatures across the nation prohibited any attempts at meddling with the magic of the land itself.

And without even that option at hand ... well, what magician with any significant power would choose to spend all his focus on reading the hidden secrets of the weather when he could be casting actual magic?

I didn't know a single one. But when it came to the question of whom I should approach tonight...

I felt Wrexham's gaze before I saw him — a prickle against the side of my neck that made me instinctively turn before I could think better of it.

He stood by the wall on my right, beyond the mingling crowd, alone and apparently content to be so. In our student days, he would have propped himself bonelessly against the wall. Now he stood erect, with a glass in his hands, and watched me steadily.

But he didn't look furious, as I'd half-anticipated, or like a man only waiting to seize any opportunity to pull me aside and lecture me on my mistakes. The look on his face as our eyes met across the room … could that really be rueful affection that I saw?

The sight pierced all of my carefully-shored-up defenses.

He'd shaved since this afternoon.

…What an idiotic thing to notice. Of *course* he'd shaved. He wasn't a scruffy scholarship student from the docks anymore.

Yet here we were again, just like that first night all those years ago, watching each other across a crowded room.

This time, unlike that memorable first evening — and thousands of other evenings since then — he wasn't striding toward me through the crowd to spend the rest of the evening at my side in lively discussion and debate. In fact, he didn't show any signs of moving toward me at all. He must have come to the conclusion that there was no use in arguing with me anymore.

Naturally, I was delighted. Utterly delighted, not to mention relieved. *Deeply* relieved.

Although … I had to admit, it *was* rather a waste to have spent so long preparing my list of brilliant justifications for this afternoon's actions and decisions, only to have no chance at all to deliver it.

As he lifted his glass to salute me across the room, the corners of his lips quirked upward into a wry grin. It was by far his most appealing expression.

My lips began to curve in return…

Horrified, I slapped one hand to my mouth. Was I actually *smiling back* at him? And coming up with justifications to *seek him out myself* later on, just when he'd finally given up on approaching me?

So much for all of my great resolutions.

Even after everything that had happened four months ago, it seemed I couldn't stop being a fool when it came to judging my own strength.

I yanked my gaze away from my ex-fiancé, breathing quickly. The room before me was a blur of color and movement, but somehow, my eyes couldn't focus on any of it.

"Oh come now," Jonathan said cheerfully. "Don't stop now! It's better than theater, watching you two moon over each other."

"I am not —!" I cut myself off with a snarl as my wits caught up with me. Taking a deep breath, I blinked the room into clarity and said with great dignity, "I'm sure I don't know what you mean."

"We should sell tickets," my brother told me. "It's like watching an opera, but far better because there's so much less tuneless shrieking involved. No, it's all wordless emoting and high drama with you two, and — *ow*!"

"You deserved it," I told him, as I pulled my arm free and he patted his elbowed side consolingly. "Amy would tell you so, too, if she were here."

"Ha! Amy would volunteer to be stage-manager, and you know it."

"God forbid," I said devoutly.

He laughed. "And speaking of my wife..." His mischievous grin shifted into tenderness as Amy sailed toward us through the crowd, resplendent in glittering gold velvet with bright silver trimmings in the overdress that parted and fell around her magnificently rounded stomach. "Darling," he said as she joined us. "You've missed the most entertaining —"

"*Jonathan!*"

"Don't tease your sister, darling," Amy said calmly as she slipped into place between us. "Unless it involves any really interesting gossip, of course, in which case I want to hear all about it immediately."

"*Amy!*"

"Good evening, darling," said my betrayer, smiling at me. "Have you spoken to Wrexham yet?"

"Not in words, so far," Jonathan told her cheerfully. "Only impressively longing glances. The air was positively sizzling between them when we first arrived."

"Oh!" Amy let out a *tsk* of disappointment. "And I missed it!"

"Don't worry," said my brother. "I'm sure we'll have plenty more action by the end of the evening. Personally, I predict a storm of broken dishes over supper and an illicit embrace in a broom closet by bedtime."

I set my teeth together. "Your husband," I informed Amy, "has the most appallingly immature sense of humor. Can't you do something about that before he gets much older?"

"It depends," said Amy, her eyes sparkling. "Can I be the one to discover you two in the broom closet? Please? I promise to scream very loudly so that he's utterly compromised and can't possibly escape."

"Ohhh!" I gave up on my incurable family. "If anyone ends up in a broom closet," I told them, "it'll be the two of you, when I lose my temper and lock you in there."

"Mm." Jonathan grinned down at his wife. "Sounds fun."

"Shush," she told him firmly. But there was an unmistakable smirk tugging at the corners of her mouth as she turned away from him. "Cassandra, I want to introduce you to somebody. A gentleman. I'm quite certain you'd enjoy sitting next to him at supper."

"I — what?" I blinked, caught off guard. "Are you match-making me with someone else now, too?"

My brother let out a low whistle that was too quiet for anyone outside our family group to hear the vulgarity. "Does he know that he'll have one of the Boudiccate's own officers of magic glaring daggers at him across the table?"

"He's a magician himself," Amy told both of us. "A weather wizard, to be exact."

Aha. My shoulders relaxed as I smiled back at her. "In that case, I'd be delighted."

"You *would*?" Jonathan's eyebrows shot upward.

"I'll explain it all later, my love." Amy patted her husband's arm comfortingly. "Now, look that way — just there — yes, here he comes." She smiled brightly as a solidly built man in his mid-thirties, with a bright crimson waistcoat and thick sandy hair, shouldered his way toward us through the shifting crowd. "Why, Mr. Sansom! You're just in time. May I introduce you to my sister-in-law, Miss Harwood, and my husband, Mr. Harwood?"

"Delighted, delighted." He gave a rough bow in each of our directions before his gaze fastened back on me. "I hear you're curious about weather wizardry, Miss Harwood. Want to learn the *real* truth beyond the pap and nonsense we're all fed at the Great Library, eh what?"

My spine stiffened, but I forced a polite smile. "Exactly."

"Harrumph!" He gave a nod of evident satisfaction. "Well, then. I'm the man to tell you all about it!"

"I can hardly wait," I murmured as I took his arm.

And I didn't have to. Mr. Sansom, as it transpired, was more than willing to pour the fruits of all his years of labor into a receptive and knowledgeable ear at long last — and as any respectably trained, practicing magician would have used all of his magical abilities to extricate himself after no more than five minutes of such rampant quackery, I supposed a famously failed and broken magician like myself must have seemed his next-best option.

Four months ago, I would have cast a spell of deafness on myself for both of our sakes. But as it was, seated next to him at one of the three long tables that filled Lady Cosgrave's dining room, there was no possibility of escape … and supper that night seemed that it would never end.

"…But then the Druids, you see, understood the worth of proper diets! No milk or bread for them, no, none of that nonsense. They intended to be *one* with nature, Miss Harwood. There's no spellcraft required whatsoever when you're already part of the earth yourself!"

"I see," I said faintly. A footman was making his way between the guests, offering refills of bubbling, popping elven wine from a tall crystal decanter; I scooped up my now-empty glass and thrust it upward in desperation. One sparkling sip later, and I could finally bring myself to ask, for courtesy's sake: "Have you had much luck, Mr. Sansom, in becoming one with nature yourself?"

"*Have* I?" Snorting, he ripped into his sliced ham with vigor. "Miss Harwood, I cannot count the number of nights in the past decade when I've felt nature's blessing of moonlight on my bare buttocks!"

I had to clap one hand to my mouth to stop wine spraying out of it. Choking, I lowered my glass to the tablecloth.

I didn't let my eyes drift for even a moment to the next table, where Wrexham sat facing me.

I didn't dare.

Oh, I had no fear that he would be glaring at my seating partner, no matter what Jonathan had mischievously predicted. If Wrexham had been that sort of brutishly jealous man, I would never have affianced myself to him in the first place.

No, what I dreaded was far worse.

I had a terrible feeling that if I met his gaze, I would discover an unholy amusement at my predicament. And then there might have to be broken dishes after all.

"Apologies for my frankness, Miss Harwood," Mr. Sansom said briskly, "but weather wizardry isn't for the weak of spirit."

"So I see." I breathed deeply as I lowered my hand. The servants' door in the far wall opened and three new footmen walked into the room, carrying large silver trays: our next course. Lady Cosgrave had apparently ordered a feast to awe the ages.

Ah, well. As long as I couldn't escape anyway... "So what do you think of our current weather, sir? As one who has such a very close communion with nature."

"Ah. Hmm. Well." He accepted a large, goggle-eyed fish and waved away the vegetables that were proffered on the side. "It is a tad on the chilly side, I grant you. But not too cold for me! No, I'll be out at the next full moon as always, and I can tell you *I* won't require any coverings."

"I understand." I looked with sympathy upon the fish, whose open eyes stared upward in horror.

The clock ticked with ominous slowness against the wall.

"Yes," I said to the footman who hovered behind me. "I believe I will have another refill, after all."

I COULD HAVE WEPT WITH RELIEF WHEN LADY COSGRAVE finally rose to signal the end of supper. The gentlemen, of course, were expected to remain at the table until a maid was sent to notify them that it was safe for them to join us in the parlor, meaning that the political conversations were officially finished for the night.

In the past, my feet had dragged as I'd followed the other ladies away from the table, abandoning the possibility of any glorious magical debates only to sit through a strategy session over the national economy in the parlor.

Now, I couldn't hurry toward it quickly enough.

"Don't worry, Miss Harwood," Mr. Sansom said as I lunged from my seat. "There is far more to explain, of course, but I'm more than happy to continue your education. Perhaps tomorrow?"

The room was ever-so-slightly shimmering around me. I blinked hard as a wave of warmth swept through my chest and head.

Tea was what I would drink in the parlor, that was it. No more wine. Possibly not ever.

I decided it was safest, all in all, not to risk a curtsy. "Thank you," I said to the weather wizard, and started for the door as gracefully as possible.

The room tilted around me with every step. By the time I emerged into the corridor, my head was spinning wildly. I only made it five feet beyond the dining room doorway before I had to come to a sudden stop.

"Cassandra?" Waiting just ahead for me, Amy frowned. "Are you —?"

"I'm fine," I said. "I just ... need a moment. Alone." Forcing a reassuring smile, I waved her ahead. "I'll be there soon, I promise."

"Very well." She rustled forward to join the other ladies as their voices dropped from the higher-pitched social gaiety of proper supper conversation to the low intensity of real political work.

They were all gone a moment later, along with the servants who'd led their way. Even their hushed voices disappeared behind the closed door of the parlor in the distance, shutting out any possible eavesdroppers. Letting out my held breath, I sagged against the wall and closed my eyes.

I needed a moment to recover before I walked on and joined them. Just one moment ... one more moment...

"Hmm," said an all-too-familiar voice close to my ear, with wicked amusement. "Rather too much joy with the elven wine, eh, Harwood?"

"Oh, shush." I slitted my eyes open just wide enough to glare at my ex-fiancé, who was leaning indolently beside me with one shoulder propped against the wall. "You would have drunk too much wine, too, if you'd been trapped in that conversation all through supper."

"What, you weren't fascinated to learn all of Sansom's great secrets?" Wrexham shook his head at me, his mischievous grin shifting into something more wry ... or even affectionate? No, that must have been the elven wine distorting my perceptions again. "I would have warned you, you know, if you'd only bothered to ask me first. I ran into Sansom at an incident up north last year, when he was chanting at the moon and ran afoul of a local group of fairies. He may be the most earnest and well-meaning would-be Druid of our age, but he certainly hasn't the power to bring about our current snowstorm."

"No one does," I said on a yawn. "That's the whole problem." The corridor shimmered in my vision, and Wrexham's strong shoulder was beginning to look dangerously tempting. If I could just rest my head there for a moment, while I regained my balance... "Even *I* never imagined that I had that much power. We're not elves, damn it, we're only human."

"That's why we work together, not alone," he said softly. "But ... ah." He let out a sigh as I shifted infinitesimally closer. "Never mind. You're tipsy on elven wine. It wouldn't be a fair fight, would it?"

"What?" I frowned muzzily at him.

Were we fighting again? No, wait, of course we were — we must be, because I'd been forcing quarrels with him for over two months now, but still...

"Shh," he murmured, as he reached out to run one long finger along the side of my cheek. "Just for once, let me help you. Just this once." His voice dropped to a whisper.

His fingers had always been so clever.

But I'd been wrong earlier, when I'd thought that his rueful grin was his most appealing expression. How could I ever have forgotten?

The intent expression he wore when he was casting magic was even better.

His spell rippled through me like sweet relief, lifting the dizziness and the beginnings of nausea like a clinging set of veils that he was drawing gently from my skin.

The unnatural warmth of the wine lifted with them. But what remained, as my head and vision finally cleared...

His dark eyes gazed into mine from only inches away, his head bent over mine, with his soft, glossy black hair falling into his face ... more than close enough to touch.

I knew exactly how it would feel against my fingers.

I had never been able to forget.

His shoulders weren't propped against the wall anymore. He was cradling me — or so it felt, although he wasn't actually touching me anymore. He had his left arm propped against the wall beside my head as he lifted his right forefinger away from my cheek.

My breath came quickly in my chest.

I wasn't dizzy anymore.

But it had been so long since we'd done this. *So unbearably long...*

His head tilted, his gaze holding mine, warm and intent and even more focused now than when he'd cast his spell. It was breathtaking. *He* was breathtaking.

He always had been.

Slowly, carefully, he shifted toward me, lowering his right arm to his side and leaving me a clear space to escape.

If I only wanted to.

Holding my breath, I rose on tiptoes...

"Ahem!" A loud cough broke the silence.

We sprang apart. I was panting, my heart galloping painfully in my chest, as I stared uncomprehendingly at my older brother ... who stood just before the open doorway of the dining room, watching us with barely-suppressed hilarity.

"*So* sorry to interrupt," Jonathan declared, sweeping an elegant bow. "But I did think I'd better warn you, in case you hadn't noticed the housemaid passing by, that the rest of the gentlemen are all about to come stampeding out here on their way to the parlor. So..." His lips widened into an outright, maddening smirk. "Don't you think you two ought to find a nice cozy broom closet before you go any further with this sort of thing?"

I stared at him, wordless, for one frozen moment. Then Wrexham shifted beside me, drawing in a breath, and I began to turn toward him —

And my reason finally, *finally* came crashing back into me.

My jaw dropped open. Heat swept through my body. But this time, it wasn't elven wine or excitement.

It was pure, unalloyed shame.

I swore that I would let him go.

If we'd waited even one moment longer — if Jonathan hadn't warned us — every gossiping magician in Cosgrave Manor would have seen us embracing and spread the news like wildfire.

Within minutes, Wrexham would have been hopelessly compromised ... and nothing I said or did after that could have released him except for our marriage.

How could I have been so careless?

With a moan of guilt, I turned and fled through Cosgrave Manor all the way to my room without a single glance back.

8

There were mornings when rising from bed to face the world seemed frankly impossible. Or even more accurately: *pointless.*

But I'd spent the last four months learning to do it anyway. So I hauled myself out of bed the next morning at a reasonable hour, I sailed down to the breakfast table with grim determination, and when I glimpsed Miss Banks's hopeful approach in the corner of my eye, I didn't even flinch.

"Of course," I said, setting down my fork as she fluttered near me. I couldn't quite summon up a smile, but I did manage a polite nod. Wrexham was just stepping through the far door into the room, but I forced my gaze to remain fixed — mostly — on Miss Banks's hopeful face. "We agreed to take a walk in the knot garden, did we not?"

"Oh, yes, if you wouldn't mind, that would be *wonderful,* although of course you can finish your breakfast first and —"

Oh, no.

For all that he was allowing himself to be delayed by

various conversational sallies along the way, Wrexham was definitely setting a course toward my table.

Grim determination was one thing. Outright heroism before I'd drunk my morning tea was quite another … and I'd learned last night just how weak my resolve had become in the two long months of our separation.

So I interrupted Miss Banks ruthlessly. "What better time than the present?" Leaving my half-full plate behind, I rose to my feet and tucked one firm hand through her arm to tow her from the room. "We may as well get this over with immediately."

Really, there couldn't be any better time to remind myself exactly why it had been so necessary to give up my fiancé in the first place … even if he was still stubbornly acting like a man who hadn't been fiercely driven away forever.

At least he didn't try to stop us as we strode, arm-in-arm, past him.

But the sardonic twist on his lips spoke volumes.

My back teeth were grinding together. I forced my jaw open with an effort as we stepped through the doorway. "We'd better —"

"Here." Miss Banks tilted her head, not quite hiding a satisfied smile, as a maid appeared at the end of the corridor with a pile of warm outerwear in her arms. "I asked for our coats and boots to be brought before I came to find you."

Hmm. There was more to the shy and sweet Miss Banks than I'd imagined. Perhaps she would survive the Great Library after all.

She certainly showed no signs of being put off by the weather, although the snow lay piled up before the house and we had to pace carefully through the narrow paths dug by Lady Cosgrave's gardeners.

A pale sun shone through the grey mass of clouds overhead, casting its watery light against the thick white snow that balanced on the branches of the sculpted hedges before us. Even more snow fell in a light, steady stream around us as we stepped through the arched opening in the hedge and into the cloistered privacy of the knot garden.

I might not be a weather wizard myself, nor one with nature, but even *I* knew it must have stopped snowing by now in any natural winter storm.

Thank goodness for the elaborately sculpted knotwork spell in the hedges. Even an elf's prying eyes wouldn't see through those branches.

Probably.

To take my mind off that disquieting thought, I said briskly, "So, what spells have you learned to cast thus far?"

"I beg your pardon?" Miss Banks slid me a startled look under her hood. "You know I haven't been accepted —"

"Yes, yes." I released her arm and pulled my own satin-lined hood more tightly around my face for warmth. "But what spells have you managed to teach yourself already?"

There was a moment's pause as she studied me warily. "You do remember that the Library directs all students to wait until their arrival —"

I waved an impatient hand. "And?"

Her expression broke into an irrepressible grin. "Look!" Whispering under her breath, she twirled around. The air shimmered.

A rainbow of lights shot up around her. Yellow, red, violet, blue...

They all speared upward and disappeared, leaving her laughing and triumphant in the snow before me. "Well?"

Something caught in my throat as I looked at her bright

young face — a knot of emotions formed by pain and piercing envy and an unexpected, fierce tenderness.

I knew that exhilaration so well.

I wouldn't let anyone take it away from this girl — not even herself.

I would *not*.

I cleared my throat with an effort. "Very good," I said hoarsely. "Very pretty. Where did you learn it?"

She blinked, looking suddenly shy again. "I ... found an old book of my father's. Well, he was going to be rid of it, actually — he never had a son, and he hasn't practiced himself in years — I think he never really cared for magic in the first place, so —"

"So you stole it," I said. "*I* see."

Her face fell. "I just —"

"Miss Banks..." I heaved a weary sigh. "Do you have *any idea* how many of my own father's books I smuggled out of his library over the years?"

"You did?" Her eyes widened.

I gave a thin smile, stretched taut by memories. Of course, I'd had it easier than she had when it came to the actual acquisition of my books — I'd had Jonathan on my side, so whenever he'd been home for the holidays I'd sent him sneaking into the family library with a list of items to procure for me. If our parents had ever caught my brother with those books, after all, they would have been only too delighted ... whereas *I'd* had them confiscated again and again whenever they were found hidden in my room, and I'd lost more than one meal as punishment for my incorrigibility.

Worse yet, after our father had died, his library door had been firmly locked ... and only Jonathan had been allowed any access to the key.

I said, firmly shoving those recollections aside, "You'll need a better book to work with. That spell comes from *Richmond's Assortment of Delights*, which is only intended for festive occasions. Lovely to pull out for a long evening with friends, of course, but not much use in practical terms. If you want to persuade the Great Library of your abilities, you'll need to prove them in a way that no one can pass off as a mere party trick."

"Oh." She swallowed visibly, looking suddenly smaller within her cloak. "I ... I'm not sure there are any other books in my house. But perhaps ... perhaps if I can find a way into Lord Cosgrave's library, or..."

"Better not steal them from our host," I said gently. "That wouldn't put you on the right foot at all. And fortunately, you shouldn't have to." As she looked at me in open bafflement, I shook my head at her. "I am *saying,* Miss Banks, that I will send you all the books that you require. I have plenty, nowadays ... and as you know, I can't use any of them myself anymore."

"But..." She surprised me by frowning with open disapproval. "What if you do need them again in the future, Miss Harwood? If you ever regain your ability to cast spells, or —"

"Trust me," I said through gritted teeth. "That won't be happening."

The look on her face was unbearable. I spun on one heel and looked across the snowy knot garden, taking deep, bracing breaths of cold air. Snow swept into my mouth and against my cheeks as I wrapped my arms tightly around my chest.

"They'll teach you at the Library," I told her, "never to cast certain spells alone. There are a few that are famously too much for just one person. And when you throw yourself into a great spell like that — when you apply all of your own power to it, as you must — it can sweep you away to your own undoing." My lips twisted. "That's what separates us from the elves, you see. Their power is intrinsic and tied into the land. Ours... We're only human. We can touch magic, if we have enough skill and enough training, but we can't always control it. We have to know our limits and respect them — or be broken."

There was a moment of near-silence as the snow fell around us in a soft, whispering hiss. A nearby hedge creaked softly as its branches bent under the weight of snow.

Then Miss Banks finally spoke, her voice quiet. "Why did you do it, then?"

More snow trickled down my cheeks, forming thin, cold paths across my skin. "I was stupid," I said flatly.

"But you're clearly not." Miss Banks stepped closer, her voice sharpening. "Miss Harwood, really. You forced the Great Library to admit you, breaking all of their previous rules and traditions. And I've *heard* other magicians speaking of you. You were the best student of your year."

"That's ... not quite fair." I winced. "Wrexham and I always battled for that top spot, actually. Depending on the year and exam, either one of us —"

"It was Mr. Wrexham who told me so, last night."

"Well." My lips stretched into a humorless smile. "That was kind of him. But." I shrugged convulsively, trying to thrust the whole formless mess of four months ago off my shoulders.

How could I explain it all to her, anyway? How everything had piled together until I couldn't breathe and I'd been ready to risk everything just to break free of the invisible ropes holding me back.

How I'd graduated with top honors, just as I'd always dreamed I would ... and then everything had suddenly *stopped.*

Oh, I'd had my magic, certainly — no one could deny me *that* anymore. I'd had all my shining awards and certificates to wave in the faces of anyone who'd dared to try. *Everyone* accepted that I was a real magician now, for all that I was back home, not at the Library anymore. And yet...

Somehow, whenever the Boudiccate had an opening in the ranks of their officers of magic, I was never, ever the one chosen to fill it, no matter how shining my awards at the Library might have been — and no matter how passionately my own fiancé fought for my inclusion after his own appointment came directly upon his graduation.

When the Great Library advertised for a new lecturer earlier this year, I wasn't even among the seven candidates invited to interview for the position, despite all the work that I'd poured into my application ... and all my articles on magical research that their own journal had published over the years.

Every time one of those articles had been published, I'd celebrated what I'd naïvely seen as a true achievement. But none of them had turned out to matter after all. Because like it or not — published or not, skilled or not — I would always be known as that singular oddity, *the woman magician* ... and apparently, not one of those awards or articles was enough to overturn all of Angland's oldest traditions and prove that I was, after all, suited for a role that had belonged solely to men for centuries.

So I'd had to do something even more magnificent. Something that would *show* them that I couldn't be ignored, left to molder in safe invisibility on my family estate with my awards and certificates while my classmates moved on to acclaim and active magical careers.

A spell that everyone knew one magician alone could never cast...

Well, everyone "knew" that a woman could never do magic either, didn't they?

I said, "Even the cleverest magician can make mistakes. Obviously."

I'd planned for Wrexham to be the witness to my triumph, to swear on it for me to his superiors. But of course I hadn't told him what I'd planned. I'd known that he would never agree to such a risk. So I'd begun the spell just before he'd been due to arrive for his planned visit, knowing that he would be too late to stop me.

And the expression on his face as he'd raced across the room to catch me, just as the spell ripped through my bones and I began that burning, tearing slide into oblivion...

I hadn't opened my eyes again for another two days after that. But when I had, he'd been the first thing I'd seen, sitting slumped by my sickbed with his head buried in his hands in unmistakable despair.

I'd known that I was risking myself when I cast that spell. But I hadn't truly understood, when I'd made the decision, just how badly I could hurt him, too.

Now I drew a deep, icy breath, letting the memory sink back through me.

I won't make that mistake again.

"What you have to understand," I told Miss Banks, "is that it isn't a matter of proving yourself once and being done with it. Being admitted to the Great Library won't grant you your classmates' respect. And graduating from it won't force anyone else to treat you the way they would treat a gentleman magician."

"Then I'll have to keep on fighting," she said. "Miss Fennell will, too." Her small jaw squared. "Don't worry, Miss Harwood. We know it won't be an easy battle. But that doesn't mean that it's not worth fighting."

"No," I said quietly. "It certainly doesn't." From somewhere deep inside me, I found a true smile. "I look forward to witnessing your achievements. And we will find you your magic books, I promise. But in the meantime..." A shiver rippled through me, and I startled myself with a laugh. "What do you say I teach you a real spell? One that can actually give us some warmth in this wretched weather?"

"Really?" Miss Banks's face lit up. "Oh will you, Miss Harwood? Please?"

Yesterday, I'd restrained myself with all my might from telling Lord Cosgrave how to cast the spell of warmth with more precision. Today, I said to Miss Banks with utter sincerity, "I would love to."

WE STEPPED OUT OF THE KNOT GARDEN OVER AN HOUR LATER, laughing and triumphant and enclosed in perfect bubbles of warmth. My cloak was steaming nicely within my bubble, and my chest felt even warmer as I watched Miss Banks dance ahead of me down the narrow path, perfectly untouched by the snow that fell around her.

It wasn't the easiest spell for a beginner to learn. But by the end, she had managed it perfectly ... and neither of our bubbles had a single leak.

If the Great Library didn't allow her in, I would eat my hat.

...And then I would eat their hidebound old selves, too! They might imagine that they could get away with accepting one woman student and then being rid of females forever, but they were wrong. I *wouldn't* be the last of us! I swore that now as I reveled in Miss Banks's delight.

I was finished with hiding. If the Great Library tried to turn her away — a girl with this much overflowing magical ability — I would talk to all of the same newspapers that had reviled me before, and I would shout and scream about the injustice until it became a story to enrage the world.

I would do whatever it took to allow a whole stream of laughing, bright young women to follow in my path and take it further than I had ever managed, and then I would —

Pop!

The bubble of spellcast warmth was gone.

Snow swirled around me as I came to a halt, frowning. Had Miss Banks's spell broken? Or —

Wait.

I jerked around, sudden panic thrumming through my skin.

A familiar silhouette stood in the distance. *Watching me.* I couldn't see his expression, but I didn't need to. The popping of that bubble had been more than message enough.

It said, *You have no protection from me.*

Everyone knew that elves liked to play games with their prey ... and more than one bubble had just been popped.

Miss Banks danced on ahead of me, unaware, just as bright and hopeful and full of potential as ever.

But as I looked after her, I felt the weight of reality settle heavily around my shoulders. Anything that I wanted to do for her or for the future of other magical girls would all have to be done within the next six days...

Because after that, I might not have any future of my own.

⁂ 9 ⁂

I knew exactly whom to consult when it came to political strategizing.

Unfortunately, Amy wasn't alone when I found her.

"My dear." Lady Cosgrave's eyebrows rose as I stepped through the doorway of the small, cozy parlor where nine ladies sat gathered in a semicircle around the fireplace with teacups and newspapers in their hands. They all looked up with bright interest as she asked, "Have you finally discovered some interest in politics after all? Your late mother would be so pleased."

I bit down a bright flare of irritation and smiled tightly. "Actually, I was coming in search of Amy, but if you're all busy —"

"This shouldn't take too much longer." Amy spoke up from the other side of the semicircle, her voice soft but her gaze intent as she studied my face. "Why don't you take a seat, Cassandra? Pour yourself a cup of tea. You can drink it while you wait."

Wait? I could feel my last six days of freedom slipping

away from me, minute by minute, like snowflakes melting against my skin.

I had to *act*.

But charging furiously around without information would be worse than useless. So I drew a deep breath and nodded, keeping my polite smile pasted to my face. "If you don't mind me overhearing..."

"*Mind* Miranda Harwood's daughter overhearing our discussion?" Next to Lady Cosgrave, an older woman with dark brown skin and grey curls, Mrs. Seabury, snorted out laughter. "My dear, if you only knew how desperately your mother *wished* you had any interest in such matters —!"

My teeth set behind my smile. I was grateful for the excuse of the tea urn in the corner, to turn my back on the semicircle of ladies and the crackling fire.

Before anyone in the semicircle could add to Mrs. Seabury's store of recollections, Amy said smoothly, "So there's still no confirmation of which representatives the elven court might send to this year's solstice celebration?"

"If any!" said Lady Cosgrave. A rustle of newspapers behind me signaled several of the ladies straightening to attention as she continued, "And when you add this dreadful weather to the equation —! It might almost have been designed to make our ceremony impossible."

My hand stilled on the copper tap of the tea urn. Suddenly, I was listening with far sharper attention.

"We're fortunate that so many of you set off early," Lady Cosgrave said. "At least five families won't be able to attend after all because of the state of the roads, and this snow isn't likely to clear any time in the next week, as far as any of the weather wizards can tell. But then, *they* never predicted how quickly this storm would begin in the first place, so —!"

I turned around, my cup still empty beneath the tap.

"How many weather wizards are at this house party, ma'am?"

"How many?" She frowned. "It's three now, isn't it? Sansom, Hilbury, and that young one, Luton, who's always growling to himself about something or other. Dreadful boy, really, but he's Delilah's nephew, so we could hardly leave him out of the invitation, no matter how unpleasant he might be."

Murmurs of assent ran around the room, and more newspapers rustled.

"Weather wizards are *not* the question at hand, ladies!" Mrs. Seabury rapped her eagle-headed walking stick hard against the carpeted floor. "There's no use hoping for a break in the storm now. The question is: will we have enough appropriate representatives of our own for the solstice circle? If there was ever a moment *not* to offer the elven court any apparent disrespect..."

More than one member of the semicircle winced.

"I can think of at least one elf who would be delighted," Lady Cosgrave said sourly. "If you ladies had seen the look on Lord Ilhmere's face yesterday..."

I abandoned my cup entirely as I moved to join the semicircle. "An elf-lord came *here*? Yesterday?"

"Not here," Lady Cosgrave said. "He would hardly deign to step into this house, I can assure you. We are *far* below his touch as mere humans, you know." She grimaced. "He can hardly bear the humiliation of our treaty, I believe, for all that it saved *both* of our nations all those centuries ago. But he was spotted on our grounds yesterday afternoon, so my husband transported me out to meet him ... as any gracious hostess should."

The look on her face said everything about the reception she had received. "He claimed he was here on behalf of his king, ensuring that everything was in readiness on our end despite the inclement weather. Needless to say, I assured him that all would be prepared for the solstice celebration ... and naturally, he didn't utter a single word of reassurance in his turn before he disappeared. But if anything isn't perfect in our circle in six days' time, I can safely swear that he, for one, will be *more* than delighted to seize upon it and present it as evidence to his king of our inadequacies as allies."

"Wait." I sank into my seat. "You're saying the solstice ceremony is in *six days' time*?"

"Keep up, girl!" Mrs. Seabury snapped. "When did you think it would be? Spring?"

"I ... hadn't thought about it at all, actually." Of course I knew the winter solstice must be coming soon, but I hadn't consulted the almanac for a date. After all, it hadn't had anything to do with me until now. No one I knew was so antiquated as to actually celebrate the twin solstices anymore — except, apparently, the elves.

Perhaps it wasn't a surprise that they were old-fashioned.

But the elf-lord's deadline to me had suddenly taken on a new significance.

If anything isn't perfect in our circle...

He was planning to confront me in the midst of the ceremony itself, wasn't he? I seriously doubted that *two* high elf-lords had been lurking in the grounds of Cosgrave Manor yesterday ... and I couldn't imagine any act more beautifully designed to disrupt a treaty ceremony than the capture and abduction of a daughter of the Boudiccate.

Lady Cosgrave might well allow me to be taken for the sake of the treaty. But it would be an outrageous slap in the face of our nation for Lord Ilhmere do it at such a moment, just as our long peace was being reaffirmed. And if the ceremony was disrupted...

"Cassandra," Amy said, "you haven't poured yourself any tea. Aren't you thirsty?"

"What?" I snapped out of my thoughts to find all the ladies looking at me with more or less impatience. "Forgive me," I said, straightening in my seat. "Too much politics and my brain shuts down, apparently."

Mrs. Seabury let out a crack of laughter. "So much for *that* bloodline! Poor Miranda. All her hopes..."

Lady Cosgrave hummed a disapproving, *"Hmmm."*

The semicircle tightened back in on itself as conversation resumed, leaving my gauche interruptions behind. I sat in invisibility-seeking silence for all the rest of it, keeping my thoughts to myself.

But I could sense Amy's gaze on me more than once in the next quarter of an hour, and I knew I hadn't fooled my sister-in-law in the slightest.

❧

JONATHAN WAS IN HIS AND AMY'S BEDROOM WHEN WE arrived, seated at the small writing table with two piles of papers stacked around him, a bottle of ink on the table, and even more blue ink smeared through the top of his thick brown hair.

Oh, dear.

"Are the footnotes really that bad?" I inquired, as I closed the door behind myself and Amy rustled into the room ahead of me.

"*What* footnotes?" Jonathan demanded. He pointed accusingly at the stacks of papers with one ink-stained finger. "*Those* are not footnotes. Those are a maze designed to drive men mad! The printers have jumbled them all out of order, and as I don't have any of my reference books here to consult —"

"My poor darling." Amy put her hands on his shoulders and dropped a kiss on his ink-stained hair. "Could you look for them in Lord Cosgrave's library?"

"Ha! That's all tedious spellbooks and magical treatises from top to bottom. As if *those* were of interest to anyone with a — no." He let out a heavy sigh and grabbed hold of his hair, tugging hard. "Forgive me, both of you. I'm just —"

"Frustrated," I completed for him as I plopped myself down on the end of their bed. "Why don't you send the journal a letter and tell them they'll simply have to wait until you've finished your visit so you can consult your own books and fix their errors?"

"And let the article be delayed *again*?" Jonathan's voice rose to a pained bellow.

"Shh," said Amy soothingly. "Dearest, I had a chat with young Miss Fennell over breakfast, and it seems she's been studying some very rare documents about the elven court in hopes of being chosen as the next ambassadress. But she's having quite a bit of trouble deciphering some of the ancient annotations, so she could do with an expert's advice and help. She's in the library right now ... and I did promise that you would take a look at them for her. You know how difficult those old manuscripts can be for people without any practice reading them."

"They're probably half-full of ancient Deniscan terms, if they're about the elven court." Reluctant interest crept into Jonathan's voice. "If they really are some of the older manuscripts, I suppose it wouldn't hurt for me just to glance through them ... although I ought to keep fighting with these damned footnotes..."

"Later," Amy told him firmly. "After you've had a chance to clear your mind. You know it always makes you feel better to lecture people about history."

"Rascal." Jonathan scooped up her hand and kissed it. "But you're absolutely right, of course. It does. And you've put up with more than enough of it already." He pushed his chair back and brushed down his rumpled waistcoat. His hair, of course, was still standing up in all directions, so Amy stood on tiptoes to pat it down as he shrugged on his dark blue morning coat, which he'd laid over the back of the chair. His lips curved into a worryingly mischievous grin as his gaze landed on me. "Everything resolved now with Wrexham, eh? Last night —"

"You are going to forget what you saw last night," I told him sternly.

"Ha!" He did up his buttons as his expression turned smug. "You can't cast any spells of silence on me now, little sister. And if you think you can glare me out of remembering exactly what I saw, in vivid detail —"

"Library!" Amy said firmly, and pushed him toward the door. "You don't want Miss Fennell to give up on those manuscripts and leave before you get there, do you?"

Shrugging, Jonathan allowed himself to be guided from the room. Just before he closed the door behind him, though, he stuck his head back in for one last comment. "I remember everything!"

"Argh!" I would have thrown a pillow at him if there had been time. But he slammed the door shut, laughing, just as I lunged across the bed to grab one.

"You two," Amy said calmly as she walked back across the room, "deserve one another."

"Oh, shush." I slumped back onto the mattress, suddenly feeling every hour of the sleep that I'd missed.

Of course *I'd* remembered every detail of last night, too … all night long. It had not been conducive to a good night's rest.

But there was no use torturing myself over that now. So before Amy could pursue the matter any further, I said, "I need your help."

"Oh?" She sat down at the writing table, arranging her skirts around her, and looked at me expectantly. "Is this about Wrexham? Or am I finally going to find out what you were angling after in that meeting? What do *you* care about the elves?"

I pushed myself upright before I could lose all of my momentum entirely. "It's nothing to do with elves *or* with Wrexham," I said firmly. "It's about Miss Banks. But not only her…"

Amy listened carefully as I laid it all out, her eyebrows drawing down with concentration. When I finished, she sat in silence for a long moment.

"You know," she said finally, "the Boudiccate won't be happy about this idea at all."

"The Boudiccate? What business is it of theirs?" I frowned at her. "They aren't the ones who train magicians."

"But they *do* run the country," Amy said patiently. "And your mother made them certain promises when she allowed you to attend the Great Library yourself."

"What promises?" I demanded. "I was never told of any!"

"Because you were doing your best *not* to notice any of the politics of it, as I recall," Amy told me. "Still, it must have occurred even to you at some point, mustn't it? One female magician could be called a rare exception. Two, though … well, that might begin to change the rules — and not just for magic."

"Oh, their blessed *rules*." I rolled my eyes. "The Boudiccate is entirely too hidebound and you know it. You would be a *part* of it, if they weren't so ridiculously attached to their traditions!" I waved an impatient hand. "How could you not tell me the real reason why you were denied Mama's place all those years ago?"

"Someone told you that?" Amy's lips compressed. She laid one hand on her rounded stomach as if to protect it. Then she sighed. "I suppose it was always bound to come out one day. But what would have been the purpose in telling you at the time? You would only have raged and kicked up a fuss and missed all of your important exams to come running to defend me — and truly, we were dealing with more than enough already, in the wake of your mother's passing. No one needed any more pain added to that moment."

"What about you?" I demanded. "You fought for me to get my place at the Great Library. Why wouldn't you let me fight for you, too, when you needed it?"

"Because it wouldn't have worked!" Amy said. "Cassandra, only *think*. The members of the Boudiccate are the proudest women in this land. Do you actually imagine they would have responded well to noise and humiliation in the public realm? Do you believe they would ever have welcomed a new member who'd been forced on them with that sort of battle? I know you like to approach everything with a battering ram, but these women require subtlety."

"And you're willing to make do for the rest of your life with that cursed *subtlety* and compromise?" I snorted. "Being part of their circle but not-quite-one of them forever?"

"Rather than lose my husband? Yes! A million times over." Amy's tone hardened. "You come from a family that always loved you, Cassandra, even when they didn't understand you. I think sometimes you forget how many advantages you have even now, even after everything that's happened to you."

I bit back an angry retort as I absorbed the look on her face ... and the undeniable sting of truth in her words.

Amy had been my mother's goddaughter since birth, but after her own parents had died, she'd been shifted from home to home among her various aristocratic relatives — too high-ranking to be fobbed off on strangers, but too inconvenient to be welcomed in any one household for long. She hadn't had a permanent home of her own until she'd finally reached the age of majority and been taken in by my mother, first as Mother's assistant and then as her political protégé.

She'd always been so good at adapting to every situation that I sometimes forgot how she'd first developed that skill. And of course, I had only been a girl when she'd arrived all those years ago. It was hard to remember now that she hadn't always been a natural, essential part of our family, negotiating between me and my mother at our worst and saving all of us from one another more than once.

I released my held breath with a heavy sigh and relaxed my clenched fingers from around the bedcovers. "I love *you*," I told her, "even when I don't understand you."

"I know you do, darling." Amy pushed herself up from her chair to join me on the bed. "I'm the only reason you and your brother both remember to change your clothing and even eat proper meals now and then."

"That's ... ah." I winced. "Well, that *is* true, of course, but it's not why I love you, and you know it." I aimed her a sidelong look as she settled in beside me. "Does Jonathan know, by the way? Why you weren't given Mama's place in the Boudiccate?"

"Oh, really." Amy shook her head at me. "Your older brother is a historian. Did you think he couldn't research the truth of that for himself? He even offered to release me from our marriage at the time."

"Ha." I bumped shoulders with her companionably. "Clearly he doesn't know you so well after all. As if you would ever let go of anyone you cared about!"

"Never," Amy agreed blithely. "You and Jonathan have been caught in my wicked clutches forever."

I tipped my head against her shoulder, clinging to the moment even as I felt the minutes tick away. More snowflakes melting against my skin...

She let out a gasp and grabbed my hand. "Cassandra!"

Frowning, I let her place my hand on her rounded belly. "What's wrong? Are you in pain? Or — oh!" Her belly bounced hard against the palm of my hand, and I jerked back instinctively.

Then my brain caught up with me. "Was that —?"

"Your new niece." Amy's face was alight with joy. "She must have wanted to greet her aunt! I've been waiting and waiting for her to finally introduce herself."

I stared at her, struck dumb. Then I looked down at her rounded belly, covered by her elegant dark green, ivy-patterned cotton gown.

Holding my breath, I placed my hand with the utmost care in exactly the same place it had rested before. Waiting.

Nothing happened.

Amy laughed. "Don't look so glum," she said. "You'll see plenty of her in just a few more months, you know!"

"Of course." I took a breath and forced myself to smile and draw my hand back as if it genuinely didn't matter.

As if I would have months to feel the baby kick, any time I wanted to.

As if I would be there when she was born.

I said, "You *are* going to help me assist Miss Banks and the other women like us, aren't you? Even if it isn't what the Boudiccate desires?"

Amy's chest rose and fell with her sigh. "I will always support you," she said, "and I would never refuse you my advice. But I'm afraid that in this particular case, you're the only one who has a real chance of convincing the people who matter. If you are truly willing to come forward and talk openly about what happened to you — which will mean swallowing your pride, Cassandra, and answering the most intrusive and insulting questions again and again, for the public to pore over at their leisure — until everyone finally truly believes that your accident had nothing to do with your sex..."

"Of course," I repeated quietly as the truth of it sank through me.

Firing off a series of letters, no matter how passionate, could never be enough to win my case. No, I would need to answer endless, prying questions afterwards from the newspapers, the politicians and the Great Library alike ... and that process had no hope of being completed within the next six days.

But I couldn't leave my sister-in-law to sort that out for me any more than I could give up the opportunity to meet my first niece in person. I *had* to solve the elf-lord's challenge, no matter what it took...

...Which left only one option, no matter how unpalatable it might be.

I would have to seek out Wrexham myself and ask for his help.

Suddenly, I wished that I had poured that cup of tea.

10

Of course, now that I actually wanted to talk to my ex-fiancé, the impossible man was nowhere to be found. I'd already looked in four different parlors and the glasshouse by the time I finally gave in, sucked in a deep breath, and pushed open the door to Lord Cosgrave's library of magic.

It was a surprisingly small and cozy room with a crackling fire and a large bay window, and four months ago, it would have looked blissfully enticing.

Now, I had to force myself to step through the doorway, bottling down every unhelpful emotion and keeping my eyes focused on my goal.

Wrexham wasn't there, but my brother was, sitting bent over a small yew wood table with Miss Fennell. Their two velvet-upholstered wing chairs were closely drawn together, and a long piece of parchment sat on the table before them.

"...So you see, *this* symbol — that line that looks so accidental, following along from the end of the word? As if the writer only forgot to lift her quill in time? *That* is the symbol for 'beware,'" Jonathan explained. He was clearly absorbed in his lecture and just as clearly hadn't noticed my arrival, even as I walked steadily towards him across the carpet. "Of course the ambassadress knew the elves would read her correspondence and diaries, so she had to code her warnings."

Miss Fennell nodded vigorously, her eyebrows furrowed with concentration. "So what she actually meant, when she let her pen trail after his name..."

"Was that he was virulently anti-human and shouldn't be trusted." Jonathan nodded. "Elves may be famously prohibited from telling direct lies, but that's never stopped them from conveying the most blatant falsehoods through a bit of careful phrasing. And one doesn't become an elf lord without learning *that* skill!

"That was one of the reasons it took so many months to negotiate our final treaty. Our diplomats, you see, had to hammer down the exact details without either offending the elves with any perceived insult — and some elf-lords, like this one, were so furious at the cease-fire that they were more than ready to take offense — *or* finding ourselves committed to wildly different agreements than we'd thought we were accepting."

A prickle of discomfort ran down my skin at those words. *Different agreements than we'd thought we were accepting...*

I'd stepped into my own agreement so easily, I hadn't even felt the noose slipping around my neck.

Miss Fennell grinned widely. "I say, this *is* rather fun, isn't it? I'd better sharpen my wits before I play this game!"

The word tore itself from my throat: *"Don't!"*

It was far too brusque an interjection, and it fell into their conversation with the weight of a rock crashing through a window. They both blinked up at me, wide-eyed.

"Cassandra?" Jonathan glanced around at the rows of glass-encased bookshelves, as if reminding himself of where we were. "What are you doing here?"

It was a reasonable question, I had to admit. I hadn't entered our family's library of magic for nearly four months now, and I'd refused to keep any of my old magic books in my room anymore. I didn't even like walking past the library in our house anymore, and Jonathan had caught me more than once taking ridiculously elaborate routes to avoid it.

The fact that he'd never so much as raised an eyebrow in response was a sign of how thoroughly my older brother understood me.

I wasn't about to discuss the matter with him now, though, especially not in front of an outsider. Instead I looked straight at Miss Fennell. "Miss Banks will *not* be happy if you're tricked and trapped in the elven court. Moreover, she urgently requires your help right here if she's to have any hope of succeeding in her own goals — for *both* your sakes — with the odds stacked so heavily against her. If you truly care for her, you won't abandon her now!"

Miss Fennell's brown eyes narrowed, and I braced myself for a return blast in her foghorn voice. When a woman planned to rule the world, she didn't often take well to direction.

After a long moment, though, she shrugged. "Hmm," she said. "I'll take that under advisement."

Well. I blinked.

Her fiancée wasn't the only one full of surprises.

Jonathan was frowning at me, though, his attention well and truly stolen from the parchment in front of him. "What's happening now?"

I sighed. "I'm looking for Wrexham," I told him. "But I

beg you will *not* make anything of that! Just let me know if you've seen him anywhere, will you?"

"Aha." Jonathan's frown eased. One corner of his mouth twitched.

I pointed threateningly at him. "Not one stray word, Jonathan!"

"I saw Wrexham," said Miss Fennell calmly. "Not half an hour ago, he set out with one of the other magicians to inspect the knot garden for Lady Cosgrave. How long does it take to check the spellwork in one of those?"

"I ... don't know," I said slowly. Garden spells had never been my specialty — nor Wrexham's, for that matter. Why on earth had he been assigned that particular duty? "Thank you, though." I turned toward the door, trying my best not to take in any of my surroundings as I moved.

It was no use. The glass on the bookcases glinted tauntingly around me in the light from the bay window. I knew what the books inside would feel like. I knew the treasures that they held.

They didn't belong to me, nor I to them anymore. But that didn't stop the longing that tightened around my chest like a vise as I finally let my gaze fall across them.

I had to clench my hands into fists to stop myself from following their magnetic pull and opening one of those glass doors as I passed.

Just one look...

If I only tried a minor spell...

I took a deep, ragged breath as I yanked my gaze away from them. *Focus.*

Wrexham.

Danger.

Elves.

"So who *was* the untrustworthy elf lord in that document?" I asked my brother, ragged desperation creeping into my voice.

I had to hear Jonathan's steady voice in my ears to cover up the whisper of poisonous temptation.

Just one small spell might not kill me, no matter what the doctors say...

"Eh?" said Jonathan, looking back up from the parchment. "Oh, that was Lord Ilhmere, unsurprisingly. I've read more than once about *him*, I can tell you. Powerful fellow, high up in the court for centuries on end, and one of the nastiest in battle too, apparently — especially when it came to human prisoners. Absolutely despises us as a species, you see, and he's brilliant at twisting his words, so according to all of the various ambassadresses, he's not to be trusted by an inch."

"How very ... useful to know," I said through clenched teeth.

The library door closed with a satisfying *thunk* behind me as I strode outside.

❦

It wasn't difficult to find Wrexham once I knew where to look. I spotted him as soon as I left the house, emerging from the knot garden beside a thin, stooped older man I didn't recognize. The snow was falling thicker than ever before me, turning them into featureless silhouettes in my vision, but I knew the moment that he recognized me.

He stopped walking with a nod to the other man, who shrugged and continued forward, brushing past me a moment later on his way back into the house. But Wrexham didn't move. He remained, waiting, at the entrance to the knot garden.

The message was unmistakable. This time, I would have to come to him.

Drawing an icy breath through my teeth, I pulled my hood more tightly around my head and started forward, hunching my shoulders against the snow.

Wrexham didn't speak a word of greeting as I joined him in the archway. But he murmured a quick spell under his breath, and the snow fell away from me, almost exactly as it had done under Miss Banks's spell earlier this morning.

...Almost, but not quite. This time, I wasn't enclosed in my own bubble of warmth. I was enclosed within his, which had opened up to wrap around us both.

The heavy snowfall, which had filled my vision only moments earlier, receded into a soft, nearby hissing in my ears, almost as distant as the house and everyone else in the world right now. Only Wrexham stood before me in the warm, spellcast circle, his dark eyes deeply shadowed in his lean brown face. Apparently, he hadn't slept well either.

Standing this close, I could almost feel his breath. All I had to do was lift a hand to touch him...

I pushed the hood off my head, shaking off the last, melting flakes of snow that had clung to it. "Inspecting the knotwork spells?" I said, and wrapped my gloved fingers around my cloak to avoid temptation. "When did *you* take an interest in gardening spells, pray tell?"

He shrugged. "They're surprisingly interesting, actually. But I have to admit, they weren't my focus." As I raised my eyebrows, he nodded toward the house behind me. "That was Lord Hilbury, you see. He wanted to take a look at the knotwork, to compare it to the patterns on his estate."

"And you came along because...? *Oh!*" I swiveled around, but it was far too late. Hilbury was long gone, and the doors stood solidly shut before us. "Hilbury the *weather wizard*, you mean." He was one of the two weather wizards I hadn't met with, yet, according to the list that Lady Cosgrave had given me earlier.

Which meant...

Something painfully sweet unfurled in my chest. I turned back to my ex-fiancé and shook my head at him. "Wrexham ... when are you finally going to see sense and give up on me?"

I'd been watching this man — either openly or covertly — for almost all of my adult life, from the moment I'd stepped into my true self at the Great Library and seen him for the first time. I'd seen him laughing, I'd witnessed him absorbed in his work, and I'd felt the staggering intensity of his focus in every aspect of my life.

But I'd never seen true desperation on his face before today, nor heard his voice as ragged as it sounded now. "*Never.*" Tipping his hands upward in a gesture of defeat, he stepped back, giving me more space within the spelled circle ... but still not separating his own bubble from mine. "You can leave me any time you want," he told me. "You can break my heart again and again, and I won't even try any more to change your mind. Last night was my last attempt. But if you think I'm going to simply stand by and let you be taken by the elves without making a single move to help you..."

His lips curved into a pained smile that made my chest hurt. "I can't," he said. "I just can't do it, Harwood. I'm sorry."

My eyes were wet, but there was no snow to excuse it anymore. As my vision blurred, my voice blurred too, turning croaky and raw. "I don't *want* to be saved by you again," I told him. "Don't you understand? *That's not what we were to each other.* I was supposed to be your equal! We were partners!"

"And you think we can't be anymore?" His brows furrowed. "Is that what this has really been about, all this time? You think I want to somehow *control* you now? Or look down on you?" He shook his head in apparent disbelief. "Have I ever acted as if I think less of you just because you can't cast spells of your own anymore?"

"Oh —!" I glared at him, dashing the stupid, useless tears away with one gloved hand. "Of *course* I don't think you want to control me. I'm not a fool! I *know* you, remember? You've always cared for people who are weaker than you. That's why you're so good at the work that you do for the Boudiccate — and why you think you have to stay with me, too, for my sake. But I don't want to be your pity-object! I can't bear it. I —"

"You," said Wrexham with furious precision, "*are* a fool."

"How dare you!" I reached out and yanked him toward me by his coat collar, glaring up at him ferociously. "I am *every bit* as intelligent as you, and you know it! I was *just* as good at magic until I lost it, and I was *just* as good at —"

"You still are!" he bellowed directly into my face. "You idiotic woman! How can you not see that? You know more about magic than most magicians five times your age! Your research and the articles that you published changed the way that magicians *all across the nation* cast their spells. You're the single most impressive person I have ever met, and *none* of that changed four months ago. None of it!"

I let go of his coat, lurching backward as if I'd been slapped. "*Everything changed.*" The words burned against my tongue like poison. "If you can't even see that —"

"The only thing that changed *for me*," he gritted through his teeth, "was that *you* finally realized I wasn't good enough for you."

"What?!" I gaped at him in genuine confusion. "What are you talking about?"

"One moment," he said, "I was coming to meet the love of my life, after three whole weeks that we'd been forced to spend apart. The next moment, I was watching you *nearly die*, and I couldn't do a single thing to stop it! Then when you finally woke up and discovered what you'd lost, you realized you didn't want to marry me anymore. Well — why should you?"

He let out a humorless laugh, his face tight. "Even that damned elf-lord could tell I wasn't born into my rank. All I've ever had to recommend me is my magic. No ancient family name, no great estate, no connections ... the *only* thing that ever drew you to me was your own magic. Once that was gone, and you could see clearly..."

"Don't be ridiculous." Something was rocketing around my head, some great revelation that I couldn't yet glimpse, but there was no way to capture it with my heartbeat thundering in my ears and Wrexham filling all of my vision. "You know I never cared about family or connections."

"Only because you had all of that already!" He closed his eyes as if he couldn't bear the look on my face. "Cassandra, your own mother was a member of the *Boudiccate*. When we met, I didn't even have a first-hand set of student robes! Do you really imagine, if you hadn't been a magician yourself, that you would *ever* have bothered to take a second look at me?"

As I looked at him then, the dam that I'd locked so firmly inside myself two months ago finally broke wide open. "Wrexham," I said unsteadily, "you *idiot*. I haven't been able to take my eyes off you ever since the day we first met!"

His dark eyes flashed open. His chest rose and fell with his ragged breathing.

I said, "I was trying to *save* you, you ridiculous, impossible man! *That's* why I fought so hard to push you away! I didn't want you to be chained to me forever just because of an old promise that you made before my magic was broken!"

"Then we've both been idiots," he breathed, "because I swear, Harwood, you nearly broke *me*. I'll beg you on my knees, if that's what it takes. Don't ever abandon me like that again!"

Unbidden, my own words to Miss Fennell rang in my ear. *"If you truly care about her, you won't abandon her..."*

I was a fool, after all, almost beyond comprehension. But I wasn't yet too much of a fool to learn from my own mistakes.

The snowfall might be thick, but it wasn't all-concealing. I darted a quick look at the house behind us, full of dangerously un-curtained windows, and then another look into the privacy of the knot garden before us. Just a few more steps, and we would be safely hidden...

No. I was thinking the wrong way again after all.

I drew myself up to my full height and lifted my chin proudly. "Wrexham," I said to my ex-fiancé, "prepare to be thoroughly compromised, if you please."

He blinked twice, rapidly. Then his lips curved. "Do you promise?" he asked. "There'll be no getting out of it this time, you know."

Oh, I knew. But I didn't bother answering him in words.

Instead, I grabbed hold of his strong, wonderfully familiar shoulders for balance, jumped up on my tiptoes, and kissed him soundly in full view of every window in Cosgrave Manor.

It was time to stop hiding for good.

11

We ended up shifting into the knot garden after all. There was such a thing as making a statement … and such a thing as much-needed privacy, too.

It had been months since I'd kissed Wrexham. *Months.*

I wanted to devour him.

But there was only so much that we could do outside in the snow, even with the protection of high knotwork hedges and the perfect, spellcast bubble of warmth around us. So I finally forced myself to draw back, panting, before we could go much, much too far.

Still, I couldn't bring myself to remove my hands from underneath his coat. I kept them tucked there like a silent claim, fingers spread against his warm, lean back as his open greatcoat billowed around us both.

Home. I had to squeeze my eyes shut for an instant to take in the perfection of that feeling.

When I opened them again, I found Wrexham looking nearly as wild as I felt, with his dark eyes wide and shocked-looking and his black hair falling around his face in haphazard disarray where my fingers had raked through it. His hands loosened their hold around me, sliding down to my hips, but he didn't let go either, even when I sank back down onto the soles of my feet.

"Harwood..." He stopped, shaking his head.

For the first time since we'd met, my ex-fiancé was apparently lost for words.

"Well?" A bubble of laughter surprised me as I took in his stunned expression. I grinned up at him, feeling every bit as young and as reckless as I'd been when we'd first met all those years ago. "You can't say I didn't warn you."

"If you had any idea..." He didn't smile back. But the look in his eyes felt like a second embrace as he lifted one hand and carefully, gently traced the outline of my face. I leaned into his touch, breathing him in. "Harwood," he murmured again.

He didn't continue. He didn't need to.

I shifted closer in to hug him tightly, laying my cheek against his chest. His heart beat rapidly against my cheek as he closed his own arms around me.

After two months apart, the relief was almost unbearable.

The idea of losing it again ... was not to be thought of.

"Well?" My voice was muffled by his waistcoat. "What did your gardening expedition teach you? *Is* Hilbury our rogue magician, do you think?"

Wrexham's warm breath ruffled the top of my head in his sigh. "Jeremiah Hilbury may well be the most cantankerous magician I've ever had the pleasure of meeting, which is an impressive feat in and of itself ... but the bulk of his ire this morning derived from the unforgivable fact that the weather is *not* behaving itself according to his firm expectations. So..." The muscles in his back shifted against my arms as he shrugged. "I believe we can tick him off from our list of possibilities."

"Then there's only one name left." I frowned, searching my memory. "*Young Luton*, Lady Cosgrave called him." Try as I might, I couldn't summon any image to accompany the name. "Do you know him?"

"Who, Luton?" Wrexham let out a huff of laughter. "I've been scowled at by him once or twice in passing, but he's certainly never deigned to engage in a conversation. I believe he considers me to be hopelessly backward, old-fashioned and deplorably chained to the establishment."

"*You*?" I pulled back to stare up at him. "Is that a jest?"

He shook his head, looking unperturbed. "I'm afraid not," he said. "I work for the Boudiccate, you see. That's more than enough to damn me in his eyes. He's quite the young firebrand in every possible regard — he even got himself sent down from the Great Library for over a year after an epic public eruption over the 'ignorance' of his teachers there. He was only finally re-admitted after his family paid a fortune to incite their forgiveness ... and even then it was only on the agreement that he would stick to weather wizardry, as none of the other teachers would agree to work with him for any payment."

Wrexham shrugged. "He is genuinely brilliant, though, from all I've heard. He could have graduated at the top of the class, just like you, and specialized in anything he'd wanted, if he hadn't been so keen to dismiss all of his teachers' own work in his final projects."

"Hmmph." In my opinion, anyone who couldn't see Wrexham's own qualities could never be described as anything close to 'brilliant.' Still...

"If he really has developed his own new methods for weather wizardry," I said, "perhaps that could account for his having such different results than any other weather wizard in history." Our teachers at the Great Library had been firm about the limitations of any human wizard's power, and those fell far short of controlling the natural world itself, even if we'd been allowed to try. Still, the weather around us spoke for itself.

...And I had no time to stand about theorizing any longer. "Very well." I nodded firmly and stepped back, pulling my hands free. "We'd better find him as quickly as possible, then, and see what we can do."

"Harwood!" Wrexham's voice stopped me just as I took my first quick stride toward the opening of the knot garden and the house beyond. When I turned back, I found him smiling ruefully down at me. "Aren't you forgetting something?"

"Am I?" I blinked.

Of course Luton might not wish to talk to us, but we would simply have to overcome that obstacle somehow. After all, we could hardly —

"*Us*," said Wrexham, shaking his head at me. "Are we betrothed again or not?"

"Oh, that." I rolled my eyes, my shoulders relaxing. "Really, Wrexham, do keep up! You have been publicly compromised, remember? I wouldn't be at all surprised if my brother has already sent out the notice to all of the London newspapers. In fact, considering all the time we've spent in here, Amy's probably planned out the fine details of our wedding venue by now. I hope you weren't expecting another long betrothal, because I doubt my family would stand for that again. They're remarkably impatient people, you know."

"I see." Wrexham's lips twitched. "Good to know. In that case..." His long fingers closed around my wrist and yanked me in. Before I could take another breath, I was pressed against his chest, all of my sensible thoughts disrupted and my heart suddenly beating with disconcerting speed while his dark, intent gaze held mine transfixed. "I've always appreciated your single-minded sense of purpose," he murmured, "but even while we're pursuing our other goals today, don't set this *too* far out of your mind, will you?"

His warm, clever lips were remarkably persuasive.

So were his hands.

My own hair was mussed and falling around my face by the time he finally straightened, and my legs felt shockingly weak. Perhaps it *was* shock, come to think of it. After all, I'd spent two long months training my body not to expect this sort of thing anymore.

I clung to the open wings of his greatcoat for balance, sucking in shallow breaths as I waited for my disobedient heartbeat to settle and my foolish legs to regain their strength. His own heart hammered a rapid beat against my wrist. I flattened one palm against it, absorbing that beat into my skin.

"You always were ... *astonishingly* good at whatever pursuit you put your mind to." My voice shivered on the words.

"Good." Wrexham sounded rather hoarse himself; he cleared his throat, his hands tightening briefly around my shoulders before he stepped back and let me go. "Don't forget it this time, if you please," he told me.

As if I ever had.

Foolish man.

But I had revealed quite enough vulnerability for one day. So I only smiled serenely and turned to sail out of the knot garden with as much grace and confidence as if I weren't still ripped half-open and reeling inwardly.

Perhaps it wasn't a surprise that I tripped. But the timing — just as I stepped out through the archway of the protected knot garden — was enough to send a jolt of cold fear like an icicle stabbing through the bubble of warmth and joy that had protected me for the past half hour.

I whirled around to peer up at the hillside beyond, where I'd glimpsed the elf-lord watching me that morning.

Nothing. It stood bleak and bare in the falling snow, and the flakes around me flew harmlessly away without ever landing on my skin. No spell had truly pierced my bubble this time. It had only been a stray branch on the ground that sent me stumbling.

Wrexham came up behind me, following my gaze. "What did you see?"

"Nothing." I forced my fisted fingers to unclench. "He isn't there ... this time."

"The elf-lord?" Wrexham's voice hardened. "You mean you've seen him again since we spoke to him yesterday?"

"Apparently, he likes to keep an eye on his investments ... and make certain they see him doing so." My lips curled into a humorless smile. Lifting my chin, I deliberately turned my back on the hills and any watchers beyond, reaching out to take Wrexham's arm and pitching my voice loud enough to be heard by anyone. "I'm sure it's all part of the amusement of the game for him. Tame housecats always like to play with their prey before they go in for the kill, don't they?"

The muscles in Wrexham's arm were rigid with tension as he gazed out toward the hills beyond with narrowed eyes, resisting my tug toward the house. His voice dropped to a dangerously low pitch, like the warning growl of a decidedly non-tame tiger. "Does Lady Cosgrave know yet that she has an elf-lord lurking about her property and menacing her guests?"

"He told her that he's here on behalf of his king, making sure that all's prepared for the solstice celebrations … which are scheduled for the same date as my own day of reckoning." I shrugged. "Apparently, Lord Ilhmere has never been a fan of our treaty."

"So he's timed all of this with great precision." Wrexham let out a hissing sigh through his teeth. Then his muscles finally relaxed, and he looked down at me with a rueful expression as he turned, following the tug of my hand. "You do keep life interesting, don't you, Harwood?"

"Just wait until you hear what I have planned for the Great Library," I told him as we started toward Cosgrave Manor and our next move in the game. "We only have to solve this one tiny problem first."

But it wasn't as easy to make progress on that matter as I had hoped.

Young Luton was apparently as contemptuous of festive conviviality as he was of the Great Library itself. He was nowhere to be found in any of the public rooms in Cosgrave Manor when we returned. Nor did he join the rest of the company for luncheon, afternoon tea or supper.

By the time the ladies withdrew from the supper table that evening, I was seething.

"Is young Mr. Luton ill?" I demanded before the drawing room door had even closed behind us. Amy had already moved toward the tea urn, where many of the younger women were gathering, but I was far too irate to care for hot drinks now. "Has anyone heard of something amiss with his health, to keep him hiding in his room all day?"

"What, him?" Old Mrs. Seabury let out a bark of laughter as she settled herself on the wing chair closest to the crackling fire. "Healthy as a horse, that boy! The stubbornest, most boneheaded ones always are, hadn't you noticed?"

A round of coughing broke out around the circle as the rest of the assembled ladies alternately averted their eyes or slid pointed looks at that oldest and crotchetiest member of the Boudiccate ... who had, indeed, existed in perfect health for as long as I had known her.

Clearing her throat and looking purposefully away from Mrs. Seabury, Lady Cosgrave said, "Delilah? Have you heard of anything amiss with your nephew?"

"What?" A vaguely familiar-looking middle-aged lady in the far corner gave a start, her teacup jostling in her hand and hot tea spilling across her lap. As she swiped frantically at the spill, I finally placed her as one of Lady Cosgrave's many cousins; no great political figure, but close enough in blood to be included in any social occasions like this one. She winced now as she looked up from her tea-stained lap and found a dozen pairs of eyes watching her. "Oh, no, has Gregory offended someone else now? *Do* forgive me! His mother swore he'd finally learned to hold his tongue in company, but —"

"Shh." Lady Cosgrave put out one placating hand. "We all know you aren't to blame for his behavior, Delilah. It was kind of you to bring him with you this time to give his poor mother some respite from his moods."

"It was *meant* to be practice comporting himself in high company," Delilah said dolefully. "My sister has great plans for him, you know, if only he could ever learn to smile and be quiet when people say things that he disagrees with. He *is* a genius, I'm told, if only we could convince anyone to hire him! But that Sansom fellow *would* keep talking of his own magical theories last night, and —"

"One can hardly blame your nephew for losing

patience," I said sincerely. "But do you happen to know where he is now? I haven't seen him all day."

"Why, Cassandra." Lady Cosgrave raised her eyebrows knowingly at me. "I would have thought you would have far more important things to worry about today of all days. Hasn't your new fiancé — or should I say, your *renewed* fiancé — been providing enough entertainment for you?" She smiled fondly as a ripple of interest ran around the circle, and the gathered ladies drew closer with a visible eagerness that grated against my taut nerves. "We're all *so* pleased that the two of you finally sorted things out after all. I always knew you would, once you overcame your little difficulties."

"Now things can finally be just as they should have been all along!" said the lady next to her. "*He'll* take care of all the magic in the family, and you can finally take your own place in politics, just as your mother always wanted. It's almost too perfect to be believed, isn't it?"

It was certainly *something.* But before I could even begin to express my full and sincere reaction to her statement, Amy hurried up behind me. Clearly, she'd sensed danger just in time.

"Are you speaking of Mr. Wrexham?" she asked brightly. "Do you know, he told me that Cassandra's articles on magic have influenced magicians five times her age! They are *so* well-matched. But I think I heard someone talking about Mr. Luton beforehand. He is a weather wizard, is he not?"

"Yes," I said tightly. "But he hasn't emerged from his room all day, as far as I can tell."

"Well, he's probably working. You've had a few days like that too, as I recall, when you were seized by some grand new experiment you couldn't wait to attempt." Amy squeezed my arm gently. "At any rate, it can't take forever, can it? I'm sure you'll have a chance to meet with him soon, once his current project is finished. And in the meantime..."

She turned to the others with a question about the upcoming solstice celebration, and I gave up and retired to the tea urn, where the younger women clustered in a gossiping group. Miss Banks greeted me with a shy smile and Miss Fennell with a firm nod, and I nodded back to both of them, finding renewed purpose in the sight of their hands brushing slightly, discreetly, against each other as they stepped aside to make way for me.

I wasn't, after all, the only one whose future was at stake.

I might have failed in my mission tonight, but I wouldn't let myself fail again, for any of our sakes. As I poured the hot, steaming tea into a delicate porcelain cup, I made a vow to myself: if young Luton didn't emerge from his room soon, I would throw propriety to the winds and go and fetch him myself.

He might have been too much for our teachers at the Great Library to manage, but after four months of broken dreams, I'd finally discovered a sense of hope again. There was no magician in the land — no matter how powerful, arrogant or obstreperous — who could be allowed to take that from me.

12

The only problem with being officially affianced again was that it was nigh-on impossible to behave like an idiot without being noticed at it.

"*There* you are," Wrexham said behind me the next morning, and I came to a sudden, horrified halt just before I could place my ear against yet another closed door in the third-storey guest wing. "Have you decided to turn yourself into a ghost for Lord Cosgrave to brag about to his visitors?" he inquired. "Pacing the halls, moaning at all hours…"

"I was *not* moaning," I said tartly. *Pacing*, on the other hand… I suppressed a wince as I took a quick step away from the closest door and turned to face my fiancé. "I was trying to ascertain which room was young Luton's, if you must know."

Wrexham smirked as he strolled toward me down the wide, carpeted corridor, looking distractingly enticing in a fitted dark green morning jacket, silver waistcoat, and soft-looking gray trousers that clung neatly to his long legs. "I'm surprised you didn't simply stand in one place and start banging on a set of pots and pans until he emerged."

"Give me credit for *some* discretion, if you please." I rolled my eyes even as I moved forward to run my hands firmly across that silver waistcoat. There had to be *some* advantages to being discovered by him in a deserted corridor, after all. I slid my arms up around his neck and narrowed my eyes at him admonishingly as I pressed myself fully against his deliciously lean, strong figure. "I don't *often* carry on sensitive discussions in full view of an entire house party, you know."

"Not *too* often," Wrexham agreed, and closed his arms around me, leaning down to nuzzle against my hair. His warm breath chased against the back of my neck as his soft hair slid against my cheek, sending shivers down my skin. "How long do we have to wait until the wedding, exactly?"

"Amy says she can have it planned within two months." I closed my eyes, breathing him in with every fiber of my being. "It couldn't be much longer than that, anyway, or we'd have to wait until after their baby is born."

"No more waiting," Wrexham said fervently. "We should never have waited so long in the first place."

I grimaced as the eager warmth inside me drained away. "You know why I wanted to wait last time." I'd been adamant that we would start our marriage as full equals; that *both* of us would have established public positions as noted magicians before we ever spoke our wedding vows.

I'd tried so hard to ensure that *no one* would ever be able to make the sorts of assumptions about me — about *us* — that I'd heard spoken aloud in Lady Cosgrave's drawing room only last night.

Of course, more than one person would say it now when they heard the news, whether or not I was there to hear it.

It was not a happy thought. Gritting my teeth, I lowered my face to hide my expression.

Wrexham dipped his own head low to catch my gaze. "Harwood," he said firmly. "You know we're equal partners in every way. It doesn't matter what any ignorant strangers imagine!"

"I know." I sighed. It wasn't Wrexham's fault, at least; I knew that much. So I stroked one hand over his warm, smooth-shaven cheek in an apologetic caress before I detached myself again, more firmly this time. "But we won't be able to be married at all if we don't sort out this problem first. And we'll never be able to do that if I can't —"

"Good *God*, will no one ever grant me a single moment of peace and quiet?!" The closest door flew open with a crash, revealing a young man with wild, un-brushed blond hair that stood out around his face like a lion's mane, and without so much as a vest or a cravat to cover his un-tucked, nearly transparent cotton shirt. "Will I *never* be allowed to focus in this blasted hellhole?"

Satisfaction rippled through me.

I put on my most gracious smile as I stepped unhurriedly away from Wrexham. "Mr. Luton, I presume?"

"Bah!" He slammed the door shut on both of us. A moment later, I heard the telltale sound of a deadbolt locking into place.

"Time to get out the pots and pans?" Wrexham suggested wryly.

"Hardly," I said. "I have something far more useful." Turning, I gave him a smirk. "You see, *I* have an officer of the Boudiccate at my side ... and I know exactly what to do with him."

It was the work of a moment for Wrexham to spell free the lock. The door swung open a moment later, revealing a room full of chaos, with scattered papers, garments, handkerchiefs, and more covering the floor like a carpet, and Mr.

Luton at the end of it all, pacing agitatedly back and forth before his un-curtained window. He stopped in mid-stride to stare at us as I strode into the room and Wrexham gently closed the door behind us.

"What the hell do you two think you're about? If you think you can march into a man's private property —"

"Lady Cosgrave's private property, actually," I said, "and she won't be happy when she discovers what your work's done to her political negotiations."

"*What*?" He shook his head impatiently. "Never mind. Just get out! If I don't get a handle on this soon —"

"Lost control of the spell, have you?" Wrexham wandered into the center of the room, inspecting the assorted elements with an apparently casual interest. His gaze passed idly across a pile of undergarments and books.

A stranger would never have been able to pinpoint the moment when he found exactly what he was looking for. But I'd been reading Wrexham's expressions for years.

Luton gave a furious start as Wrexham plucked a single piece of paper from the pile. "Don't you dare touch my notes, you Philistine!"

"'The process of bringing about unnatural snow,'" Wrexham read aloud. His eyebrows rose slightly as he read silently down the rest of the page. "Interesting. I wouldn't have guessed at some of these..."

"You ignorant ass! You have no idea what you're talking about. Bloody *typical* establishment arrogance! Here." Holding out a peremptory hand, Luton snapped out a spell I recognized — but the paper didn't budge from Wrexham's fingers. Instead, as Wrexham continued to read the page with calm concentration, the backfire from Luton's spell sent the younger man skidding backward across the cluttered floor.

He had to catch himself on the windowsill behind him … and I didn't even try to restrain my smug smile as I watched him struggle to recapture his balance while staring at Wrexham with open shock.

So much for condescending to my fiancé!

Unlike some magicians, Wrexham had never bothered to brag about his abilities. *He* didn't need to. Unlike Luton, he hadn't had a wealthy family to buy his way into the Great Library — only his own fierce talent and ambition, which had won him his deserved place over other men who were far higher-born and better-connected.

And it was remarkably satisfying to watch Luton take in the full force of his misconceptions.

But the shock on the younger man's face didn't last for long. He scowled as he righted himself, releasing the windowsill with a low growl. "Damn it! Wrack — Wreck — whatever the hell your name is — I'm in the midst of the most important work of my life! Can't you see that?" He braced himself like a bull, shoulders lowered, preparing to rush forward for a physical attack. "You may be too stodgy-headed to understand, but if you don't let me finish without any more interruptions —"

"Not a chance," I said firmly as Luton slammed into an invisible wall several inches from my fiancé and went crashing to the ground. "Trust me," I told him, stepping forward to look down on his prone figure, "I don't care for the one elf-lord I've met any more than I care for you on first acquaintance — but we still can't allow you to break our treaty. It's kept this nation and our people safe for centuries, and we will *not* stand by while one arrogant boy breaks it for his own selfish reasons."

"You think *I've* broken a treaty?" Rolling over, he stared

up at me from the floor where he'd landed atop a pile of crumpled cravats and coats. "Are you mad?"

"Harwood," said Wrexham quietly, "I think you'd better read this list before you go any further. I'd like your opinion on it, if you please."

"Hmm." I twitched it out of his hand and frowned as I read impatiently down it. One method after another ... and another ... and another ... "But these are contradictory," I said. "They would never work together."

"Of course not!" Luton snarled. "None of them worked in the first place, as you'd know if you knew *anything* about weather wizardry outside of the meaningless nonsense that's babbled at the Great Library and —"

"Clearly, *something* worked," I said to Wrexham, ignoring the continued snarling from the floor beneath us. "But if it wasn't any of the methods on this list..."

With a whisper of a spell, Wrexham raised his head. Every piece of paper in the room lifted itself carefully from beneath piled clothing and books and flew in a shower like white, fluttering snowflakes through the air to his waiting hands.

Luton crossed his arms, settling himself into his position on the floor with what looked like grim satisfaction. "There's no use in looking through those," he informed us. "Not unless you want to batter at your own heads as much as I've battered at mine these past few days. I'm nearly there, though, or I could be — if I could ever get uninterrupted time to bloody *think* in this madhouse!"

Wrexham shuffled through the pages, his frown deepening.

I didn't even try to read over his shoulder. Instead, I met the furious, trapped gaze of young Luton.

I knew that fury all too well. I recognized it with every

instinct in my body ... and it sent a sick certainty sinking through my gut.

My shoulders sagged as I gave in to reality.

"You didn't cast this snow spell after all," I murmured. "Someone else did, didn't they? And it's driving you wild that you can't even understand how it was possible."

"I *will* work it out," Luton gritted through his teeth. "Damn it! If one of those hidebound traditional idiots can do it despite everything we were ever taught, then *so can I.* And when I do, everyone at the Great Library will have to admit that they were fools about me *and* about weather wizardry! If I could only..."

But I didn't wait to find out what he *only* needed in order to accomplish the impossible. I'd made more than enough of those statements myself, this past year, to learn the true value of all of them.

I turned for the door, unable to speak.

Wrexham lingered a little longer, his voice steady as I closed my cold fingers around the door handle. "In your professional opinion, Mr. Luton, could a magician who isn't a weather wizard have done this?"

Luton's bark of laughter was ragged with frustration. "Do what the Great Library claims to be impossible, you mean? What every weather wizard who's trained all their life could never manage, even working *en masse*? You really are mad, aren't you?"

No, he wasn't. But we were rapidly running out of options...

And my own time was running out.

13

After two endless months in which the rest of my life had seemed interminable, my final days of freedom slipped away with dizzying speed. I had never written so many letters as I wrote in those few days, pouring all of my fury and despair into my arguments — to the Great Library itself, and to every newspaper and every magician I could think of who might be swayed by the thought of those magical girls and the education they so richly deserved.

But I didn't post any of my letters. Not yet. Any such flurry of activity would have alerted my sister-in-law to the fact that trouble was brewing — and she was safely distracted at the moment, between assisting in Lady Cosgrave's preparations for the solstice and planning my own projected wedding.

I saved all of my letters in a closed drawer in the little dressing table in my room, along with more notes addressed to my closest relatives, placed on top where they could be most easily discovered. I might not be sharing the news of what was coming with Jonathan and Amy, but there were some truths that I had to write down for them anyway, for them to read in the aftermath.

Heartfelt thanks had to be given. Heartfelt apologies, too.

...And there was one more relative I still had to address. I couldn't write any given name atop that particular note, but I signed it in my most elegant handwriting, *with love from your aunt Cassandra,* and I gritted my teeth to keep my jaw from trembling as I sealed the folded paper with one decisive stamp.

It was past midnight on the night before the Winter Solstice. There was no time left for tears.

I might have wasted the last two months of my life in bleak despair, but I wouldn't waste another moment of it now.

Wrexham opened his door even before I'd finished tapping my fingers lightly against it. The still and silent corridor was dimly lit at this time of night, with only a few fey-lights left glowing to aid guests in their nighttime perambulations. Still, my fiancé was fully dressed in his evening attire, with dark stubble creeping across his lean brown face.

"You've had a new idea?" he whispered urgently. "Or —"

"Shh." I slipped inside and locked the door carefully behind me. A brace of candles stood atop the desk in the far corner, and I could see a pile of books set nearby; he'd obviously been poring over them when I arrived.

"We have to be quiet," I whispered. "I don't want Amy and Jonathan to be embarrassed by anyone discovering me here." I'd created enough social challenges for my family without adding any more to my list at the very end.

Nodding, Wrexham whispered a spell that hummed through the air before closing us in a protected bubble. "No one will overhear us," he said in his full voice. "So tell me: what have you discovered?"

Fury and panic and despair had mingled so intensely within me over the past few days that I'd often felt as if I might explode from the sheer force of them. But as I looked at him now — my brilliant, driven fiancé, his eyes shadowed from the nights he'd spent fighting to find a way to save me — warmth filled my chest and washed all the rest away.

I'd thought I had lost everything four months ago. I had been so wrong. And realizing that in this past week was the most bittersweet gift that I could ever have been granted.

So: what *had* I discovered?

"That I have no more time to waste," I said with soft conviction, and I started toward him.

Wrexham frowned uncomprehendingly as I pulled off my evening gloves and let them fall to the floor. "What do you mean?" he said. "Are you — mmph!" His eyes flew wide open with rare shock as I cut him off … and not with words.

I loved talking with Wrexham more than almost anything in the world.

But tonight was my last and only chance for more, and I wouldn't give that up for anything.

We were illicitly and delightfully tangled on his bed ten minutes later, laughing and giddy with shared delight, when he suddenly pulled back, panting hard, and stared down at me. His shirt was off by then, revealing delicious, warm brown skin and shockingly soft dark hair that curled invitingly against my questing fingers. I wanted to explore every inch of it, but he shook his head at me, his long, black hair slipping over his face as he supported himself on his fisted hands.

"Wait a minute," he gasped. "We have to think this through. We can't — we don't have time for —"

"We don't have *time*," I agreed fervently, and reached up to cup his beautiful, beloved face in both of my hands. "Wrexham, I *have* thought. Trust me, I've done nothing *but* think all through this past week, and so have you! We aren't going to solve this mystery tonight, or find a way to break my promise without breaking the treaty."

"Curse the treaty," Wrexham snarled. "We'll just leave, now —"

"And let the whole nation suffer for it? Really?" Emotion welled up inside me as I saw the torment in his expression. "You're an officer of the Boudiccate," I said softly. "You know we cannot let that happen. No, I made a promise to the elf-lord's pet, and now I'll pay for it ... but then you *will* find a way to *get me back* if it's humanly possible. Won't you?"

Wrexham clenched his jaw and didn't answer ... but the muscles in his bare arms, which were braced around me, tightened in a way that was entirely distracting.

"Listen to me!" I told him in my most peremptory tone. "I threw away the last two months that we could have spent together. But now, at least, *we have tonight.* Are you really going to waste it hurling curses at Lord Ihlmere? Or are you finally going to make some use of the time that we've been given?"

"*Make some use?*" A gleam of humor appeared in Wrexham's eyes. A sigh rippled through his body ... as it lowered infinitesimally toward me. His warm chest brushed against mine.

I caught my breath, every muscle in my body tightening with anticipation.

"Was that a challenge, by any chance, Harwood?" my fiancé inquired in a silky, dangerous tone.

Satisfaction rippled through me as I arched shamelessly toward him, savoring every single point of connection.

"You've met every challenge in your life so far," I breathed. "Why don't you do it this time, too?"

He did.

I didn't manage much sleep that night, but my body still hummed with warmth and sweet, unfamiliar sensations as I arose the next morning from my own bed, to which I'd finally returned. Flashes of memory accompanied me like fleeting shadows behind my eyelids, overlaying each moment as I moved — Wrexham's strong, sensitive fingers stroking with aching tenderness across my skin; his expression as he'd gazed up at me...

I blinked again, and my vision was ruthlessly clear.

The curtains had been opened while I slept. Snow fell beyond the windowpanes in an endless white flurry, too thick for me to even glimpse the rugged hills and massive, sleeping trolls who lurked beyond.

Somewhere out there in the midst of that unnatural storm, Lord Ihlmere himself was certainly waiting for his moment. The only question, now, was exactly how I would choose to give it to him.

I had come to a new conclusion last night after all, in the midst of that warm, enchanted bubble of privacy and exploration and unimagined possibilities.

I'd cast that final, catastrophic spell on my own four months ago to prove to myself and to everyone else that I was too strong to ever need any help. Then I'd driven Wrexham away for his own good two months later ... or so I'd told myself at the time. But in the end, I wasn't the only one who'd been punished by that misguided decision.

There were perfectly good, persuasive reasons not to tell my family the truth of what was happening today, and I'd let those reasons guide every one of my decisions over this past week. But in the middle of last night, as I'd opened myself completely, one final, unexpected consideration had blossomed within me ... and in this morning's clear, unforgiving light, it overwhelmed all the rest.

I wouldn't shut out the people I loved anymore. *That* wasn't strength or courage after all. And if I only had a few hours left of freedom, I refused to spend them giving in to fear once again.

I was carrying my three final, personal letters with me when I tapped on Amy and Jonathan's door a few minutes later. They felt slippery in my hands as I fidgeted, my feet shifting against the carpeted floor and my own breath loud in my ears. A pair of guests passed behind me: Mr. Luton's aunt and a friend, from the sounds of it, murmuring together. I didn't bother to turn and greet them. I was too busy with my own internal calculations.

If my family was already downstairs, should I bring the letters down, too? I couldn't simply slip them under the door; that would be cowardly. And yet...

The door swung open, and my older brother grinned down at me. "Hello, sleepyhead. I didn't see you at breakfast." He stepped aside, resplendent in unusual finery: his best forest-green waistcoat, a non-crumpled cravat, and hair that had clearly just been brushed. "Come in, come in. I've just been regaling Amy with some fascinating new details I gleaned from Miss Fennell's scrolls."

"Delightful," I said, as dryly as I could manage. I closed my hands harder around my letters as I stepped inside.

Amy was changing her earrings at the dressing table, but she aimed a bright smile at me in the mirror. "Hello, darling! Do you think these ear bobs look appropriately festive for the solstice ceremony? I may be dragged in as a substitute after all if Lady Frampton doesn't make it through this dreadful storm."

"That's just as well," I told her. "You know she'd only spend the whole ceremony sniping back and forth with Mrs. Seabury. They'd probably offend all the elves past bearing."

But if Amy was actually going to be there to watch...

My fingers squeezed tight into fists, crumpling my letters.

"Fair point," said Jonathan breezily, as he rearranged a cufflink on his wrist. "But I have been warning Amy, you know, not to let herself get dragged into any private conversations with the elves while she's there. It's just as I was telling Miss Fennell yesterday, you see — they're infamous, especially the elf-lords, for being able to twist their words so well that they can persuade you into foolish bargains if you aren't careful."

"Ahh ... gghl..." The words I was trying to form turned into a tangle of discomfort in my mouth.

Both my brother and sister-in-law turned toward me with expressions of bright interest.

"All right there, old girl?" Jonathan inquired, raising his eyebrows. "Need a sip of something to clear your throat?"

Amy said, "What *are* you crumpling in your hands, Cassandra? If you were meaning to post those letters, you might want to flatten them out a bit."

I loosened my fingers with a jerk, smoothing down the wrinkled pages. "These ... are for you, actually." I thrust them forward, bracing myself.

"For us?" Amy's eyebrows drew into a frown. She didn't move. "Why would you write letters to us?"

"Not only to us," Jonathan told her, as he scooped them out of my hand. He held up the letter addressed to my young niece, his voice hardening. "Apparently, she's planning to be gone for a while."

"What on earth —?" Amy began.

"Just read them!" I snapped, and strode past them both to the window, sucking in a deep, panicked breath.

This was *exactly* the kind of conversation I hated most.

The snow swirled outside as discontentedly as my own frantic, whirling thoughts. My fingers tapped impatiently against the iron-bound windowsill.

It would have been *so much* easier to stride directly out into that terrible storm and face whatever was coming to me on my own, rather than having to endure this agonizing truth-telling session first ... followed by the certain wrath of the Boudiccate afterward.

When they all realized exactly how I'd let myself be tricked through my own pride and arrogance into accepting that impossible, poisoned bargain from Lord Ihlmere...

Wait.

My mouth dropped open.

My fingers stilled.

Inside my head, the frantic storm whirled to a sudden, frozen halt.

"*Cassandra*," Amy said behind me in a strangled voice. "You —"

"No!" A wide, disbelieving smile bloomed on my face as I spun around to face my family. It stretched and stretched until I was beaming like the sun at their horrified faces.

"Forget everything I said in those letters," I told them. "I *can* solve this puzzle after all. But first: I'll need as many people there to witness it as possible."

14

It had been over a decade since the last time I'd attended an official Boudiccate ceremony. That last time, I'd stood prickling with resistance behind my mother with every inch of my body braced against the path she'd laid out for me.

That moment seemed a very long time ago, although I could see its memory reflected all around me in the faces of the older women who surrounded me now. They'd always commented on my resemblance to my mother.

She should have been here today leading all the rest, but that was an old — albeit aching — grief. My stomach might be roiling with sick tension now, but Amy and Wrexham walked on either side of me in the center of the crowd, while Jonathan walked so close behind that I could feel his steady warmth against my back. My easy-going older brother had bellowed at the top of his lungs this morning and nearly torn his hair out with his agitation — and Amy had made it *very* clear, in her softest and most ominous tones, that if I did somehow manage to survive this ceremony, she would have a *very great deal indeed* to say to me afterwards about keeping vital secrets from my own family members, who deserved *far* more respect and consideration and could perhaps have even *helped* me beforehand if I had only bothered to include them...

But she had cut herself off there with a visible effort in order to preserve all the rest of the time we had left for strategizing with the full force of her wily political brain. So it was because of my sister-in-law's machinations that now, as we stepped *en masse* out of Cosgrave Manor, nearly the entire house party trailed after us through the knee-high snow, rather than the paltry nine-person committee that had originally been planned.

They would either be the audience that confirmed my victory to the world ... or the witnesses as I was dragged away forever.

Lady Cosgrave looked physically pained as she shepherded our unwieldy group into place on a wide patch of nearly-cleared ground just past the knot garden. A bubble of magic protected all of us from the elements, but her voice grew more and more strained with every moment. "If everyone could *please* ensure that we stay in two clear semicircles, with every guest who isn't an official member of today's ritual remaining safely in the outer ring ... no, *not* there, Mr. Sansom," she added sharply as the scarlet-coated weather wizard tried to bluster his way into the center of the smaller, inner semicircle. "If you please...!"

Even through my own churning nerves, I felt a moment of pure sympathy break through. This couldn't have been how she had ever imagined her exquisitely-planned ceremony proceeding.

Standing just in front of me and leaning on her walking stick, which she'd planted firmly in the snowy ground, Mrs. Seabury let out a sharp crack of laughter. "Be grateful for small mercies, girl," she called over to Lady Cosgrave. "At least Sansom's kept his clothes on for this one!"

"I *beg* your pardon, Madam." Sansom glowered at her as he allowed himself to be shuffled back into the outer semicircle with the rest of us. "If you had any conception of the infinite mysteries of weather, which occasionally require —"

"Will everyone *please be quiet*!" Lady Cosgrave's voice rose to a shriek. A stunned silence fell across the entire house party as our hostess, bereft of her customary poise, cast a desperate glare across our imperfect semicircles, her face pinched white with tension beneath her luxurious satin hood.

"Do you have *any idea* how much rides upon this ceremony?" she demanded of the company at large. "If they can seize upon a single excuse to claim insult — if a *single person here* coughs or speaks at the wrong moment — *if* Miss Harwood's rash bargain hasn't doomed all of us already —!"

I winced, but for once, I didn't argue. Every muscle in my body was braced for the oncoming battle. From the moment that I had stepped outside into the cold, snow-swept air, all the intellectual excitement of my earlier breakthrough had been replaced by an overwhelming awareness of everything that could go wrong. That list mounted higher with every moment, clenching the muscles in my back tight with dread and sending nausea rocketing through my stomach.

It didn't matter that I was certain I was right. I'd been certain I was right four months ago, too. And what had happened then, after all of my great plans...

A deafening roar of sound crashed through the air, and a towering tidal wave of snow erupted in the landscape before us.

"RAAAAAAAAAAAAARRRRRRRGGGHHHH!"

I clapped my hands to my ears, but it wasn't enough.

Nothing could be enough to protect me from *this*. The roar echoed agonizingly on and on, growing impossibly louder and louder, pounding at my head and battering all my senses until I had to fight the urge to drop to my knees in pure submission and terror. A wall of unbroken white billowed before my eyes, piling higher and higher beyond our fragile bubble of spelled protection, while the roar...

No, wait.

It wasn't a roar, after all. It was *roars*: a multitude of them, all sounding together and coming from all around us...

...From the massive, rocky hills that dotted the rugged northern landscape, all bursting upward from the ground at once.

How many ancient trolls had been sleeping there for centuries?

They were all wide awake now and advancing on us through the snow with massive, stone-strong legs. As the cloud of snow they'd flung off from their grassy sides finally collapsed to the ground beyond our bubble, I could see exactly who had woken them.

Apparently, we weren't the only ones to have desired extra witnesses to this meeting.

The elf-lords rose from the center of the white landscape, tall and beautiful and shining like icicles encased in flesh. Their long, pale hair glittered with razor-sharp shards of transparent glass. Their floor-length white coats shimmered with iridescent silver embroidery. The crown of the elf in the center looked as if it had been fashioned from pure diamond, and an audible gasp ran through the inner semicircle of human watchers as the snow cleared to reveal him.

The elven king, according to Amy, had *never* attended

this ceremony. That was the duty of his representatives, hardly suited to the eminence of his role in the elven court...

But the eyes of the elf-lord on the king's left side gleamed with unmistakable satisfaction as his cat-like gaze turned directly to me.

Lord Ihlmere was ready to claim his prey.

"Your Majesty. We are honored indeed by your presence here today." Lady Cosgrave stepped forward and bowed her head to the elven king with perfect grace, ignoring the gigantic trolls who continued to close steadily around our tiny semicircles. Even as their massive strides shook the earth beneath her feet, she kept her steely social smile fixed to her face.

"...And my lords." She looked deliberately around the assembled elves. "How delightful to see so many of you gathered in friendship for this year's solstice ceremony ... especially after such a disappointing absence from this year's Samhain celebrations. If only we'd known how many of you would be arriving today, we would have set out even more places at our feast to welcome you as kin."

A ripple of expressions ran across the faces of the elven courtiers, ranging from skepticism to outright sneers. The elven king himself, standing still and poised in the very center, appeared to be perfectly unmoved by any such trivial emotion, except...

Had that been a warning twitch of his eyebrow as he nodded gravely back to Lady Cosgrave? I frowned, peering at them both from my position at the back of the second semicircle. I was too far away and too untutored to read the intricacies of the code, if there was one, that had passed between them in that moment.

But I remembered what Amy had told me: *"It was either a deliberate snub, in which case our treaty is in grave danger —*

or else a sign that their own court is in such disarray that he didn't trust any one of his courtiers to meet with us in public this year..."

The elven king might be here to defend the treaty. But in this particular meeting, he could well be overwhelmed by his own attendant numbers ... and I wouldn't be surprised if Lord Ihlmere had more than one upset in mind for today.

"Our noble king," he'd murmured in a tone of pure venom all those days ago, as his sole reason for leaving the lost travelers unharmed.

Ihlmere stepped forward now, taking control as easily as if he'd already slipped the crown from his ruler's head.

"Alas," he said in a tone that reeked of satisfaction, "not every friendship can last forever. And when one side is guilty of such a vast betrayal..."

I wasn't the only human who stiffened at those words. Every politician in the inner semicircle sucked in a preparatory breath, while every magician in the group went as taut as a hunting dog waiting to be set loose.

My own magic should have been a vital part of our defense ... but for once, that bitter seed had no chance of taking full root in my chest. It was overpowered by the cold certainty that we would *still* have been hopelessly outmatched. Lady Cosgrave had prepared for a political ceremony today, not a battle.

Everyone knew what had happened in our last, epic battles with the elves, when our nation *had* prepared with all its might. The blood shed then, on both sides, was a nightmare passed down all the centuries.

"We share this land," Lord Ihlmere said, "but we *do not* alter it, on either side. To call down an unnatural storm such as the one that currently torments our pets and threatens our own traditional hunts is an abomination that spits in the face of our longstanding treaty. And when it comes to the human who made a promise to one of our own — a daughter of the Boudiccate herself..."

He smiled at me with glittering intensity.

"Well, woman? Have you identified and brought us one of your own, for the culprit to be punished by our laws? Or are you ready to join me for my own private hunt ... as I am *certain* your friends and family will allow without a word of protest, for the sake of protecting our precious treaty?"

Beside me, Jonathan sucked in a breath through his teeth. Standing in the circle before me, Amy lifted her chin. At the edge of the outer semicircle, Wrexham's posture was as stiff as a bayonet.

I stepped out of my place, leaving all of them behind.

My mother, if only she were here, could have warned Lord Ihlmere of exactly what ultimatums and threats did to my resolve.

All of the fear had drained out of me when he'd threatened my family. Now I glared back at him with every bit of the fury and contempt that I felt. "I won't break our agreement," I told him sweetly, "any more than my nation has."

His eyebrows rose in open disbelief. "How ... very ... noble of you." He looked around, drawing his companions into the conversation with a sweeping gesture. "So? Which of your compatriots have you brought to face our justice? Or are you turning yourself over now without any resistance? Because as you know, any resistance whatsoever from *anyone* in this gathered group —"

"Yes, yes," I said, and flicked one hand at him in dismissal as I turned to the elven king in the center of their group. "Your Majesty," I said, "may I repeat the terms of my agreement with Lord Ihlmere?"

Every other elf in the group had stiffened at my disrespect to their spokesman.

But the elven king tilted his head, his attention piercing. "You may," he said in a voice like sparkling ice. "We are listening."

"Thank you." I smiled.

I had never been a good daughter of the Boudiccate. I would never, ever follow in my mother's political footsteps.

But I knew how to memorize and recite a spell, word-for-word, without a single shift of intonation.

"I agreed," I said clearly to the whole gathered group, "to protect the elves' pets by discovering the one who cast this unnatural storm, whether the perpetrator was human or not."

"And?" Ihlmere snapped. "Have you brought him to this gathering? Or do you officially declare forfeit to me now?"

"No, I didn't bring him," I said, and kept my gaze on the king. "*You* did, Your Majesty."

A hiss of sucked-in breaths sounded from both groups.

Lady Cosgrave's face was bone-white. The elves, glittering and undefeatable, were glaring at me *en masse,* the magic that they carried within them building like a second storm and thickening the air all around us with menace.

But as I watched, one corner of the king's mouth unmistakably curved upwards. "Indeed?" he said coolly. "Do explain. To *all* of us, if you please."

"Humans lie, and we all know it!" Lord Ihlmere started forward, shining with fury. "You cannot trust any human to tell the truth, or —"

"But you can trust an elf-lord, can't you?" Jonathan said behind me. His voice came out as easily as if he were engaging in intellectual debate, and when I looked back, I found him in a relaxed pose, his arms crossed and head tilted with scholarly interest. "Isn't it true, my lords, that you never lie?"

"Never," snapped the elf-lord on Lord Ihlmere's left, his eyes narrowing. "Any such abomination would be identified immediately by every other member in this group. We can *all* attest to the truth in each other's words."

"Well, then," Amy said, from the inner semicircle. "Why don't you tell us, Cassandra, *exactly* what Lord Ihlmere said to you? And he may tell us all whether you're repeating his words correctly."

"Of course." I bowed respectfully to the group around me. "Lord Ihlmere," I said to the gathered elves and humans, "claimed that the laws in his kingdom utterly prohibit any such atrocity of nature as this spelled storm — and that it is your kingdom, not our nation, that is most harmed by it, as it has injured your pets and ruined your hunts. Therefore," I finished, "he pointed out, as I recall, that *any observer with a shred of logic* would tell us that one of our own magicians must be the ones directing all of it."

"Well?" The king turned his clear, cold gaze upon his elf-lord. "Is the human lying? Yes or no?"

Ihlmere's words sounded as if they'd been ground out through his sharp-edged jaw. "No," he said harshly. "*Which is why* any elf lord in this group, unlike a human magician, would never cast such reckless magic as an experiment!"

"As an experiment? I don't think so." I tilted my head. "But in order to break our treaty … and perhaps win yourself full power, too?"

For the first time, the group of elves broke formation. Heads turned. Booted feet shifted.

Suddenly, there was a space between Lord Ihlmere and his fellows.

"I expect there's been a great deal of unhappiness in the

elven court," said Miss Fennell knowledgeably, from her space in the outer semicircle. "Based on *my* reading, I would guess that a good deal of blame has probably been cast about in this past se'nnight. Perhaps a few questions might even have been raised about the fitness of a ruler who wouldn't step up to defend his realm when mere humans were causing such disruptions?"

"And our own disruptions," Lady Cosgrave added sharply, "were all to the detriment of this particular ceremony. This sudden storm, so carefully timed, made it nearly impossible for all of our intended attendees to gather ... as I recall *you* noting, Lord Ihlmere, in your unexpected visit to us last week."

More elves stepped away from Lord Ihlmere.

One of them shook his head in open shock. "Without our hunts..."

"I cannot believe any of you would listen to human slander!" Lord Ihlmere spat. "You know they care nothing for the truth. You *know* —"

"*I* know how good you are at twisting it." I took another inexorable step forward. "You chose your words very carefully last week, didn't you? You said that *any observer* would tell us that a human magician must be behind it all. But you aren't just any observer, are you? You're the architect behind it all."

"*You* did this?" demanded the single elf-lord who still stood beside Lord Ihlmere. His pale face was gaunt with horror as he stared at his fellow lord. "*You* hurt our pets until their cries haunted all of our dreams? You *disrupted our hunts*? You *know* —!"

"You have no proof!" Lord Ihlmere snarled. "None beyond the words of this demented monstrosity of a human female, whose bones reek of a magic she should never have been allowed to share! She doesn't even deserve to stand here among us, or —"

"I shall *not* take her word as proof." The elven king stepped forward with every other elf suddenly behind him, a flanking army of glittering and unmistakable power. "I shall take *your* word before this assembled company, Lord Ihlmere.

"Highest and oldest among our advisors. Most mighty and most proud, across the centuries." His gaze flicked across the elf-lord's enraged expression, and his narrow lips twisted. "You will answer us all and in one word only. *Did* you summon this enchanted storm, breaking the ancient laws of our realm and putting every one of our company in mortal peril?"

Lord Ihlmere swept one hand through the air in a furiously cutting gesture. "Cannot you see how we've been weakened? Human corruption and influence unbounded and —"

"Lord Ihlmere!" White light flared out from around the king's skin as he took another gliding step forward. The rest of the elves moved with him in perfect, sinuous synchronicity. "*We await your answer.* Did you betray your kingdom?"

"There is no betrayal in protecting it from enemies!" said Lord Ihlmere. "I sought only to bring us back to greatness! To —"

"The answer," said the elven king in a clarion voice, "has been given."

A sigh rippled through the elves behind him. Then the gathered elves glided outward until they formed a perfect circle around Lord Ihlmere, who stood like a trapped wolf, searching for escape.

The trolls closed in around them with earth-shaking

steps, their great heads tilted and stony gazes fixed on the elf-lord who had betrayed them.

I didn't dare release the breath that I held in my chest.

"Lord Ihlmere," said the king, "by our most ancient laws and rites, you are banished. You are lost to your brethren and to your land. The soil will not shelter you. The air will not sing to you. You are broken, root and branch, from our tree."

"You — *she* —!"

With a sudden surge, Lord Ihlmere broke through the elven circle. His beautiful face contorted in rage. He threw up one ice-white hand and pointed it straight at me.

Wrexham threw himself between us, his own arms rising and his lean form beautiful and deadly: my fiancé, determined to save me this time after all.

But this time, he wasn't alone.

Every magician in the group lunged into place behind him without an instant's hesitation ... even scarlet-coated Mr. Sansom, the obnoxious young Luton, and young Miss Banks with her chin held high, hectic color in her cheeks, and her slim arms thrown up into exactly the right position. She'd been reading the books that I'd found for her, this past week.

Even together, the whole group wouldn't be enough to stop him. But a warmth that had nothing to do with magic filled my chest as I looked at the protective wall they'd formed in front of me:

My old classmates.

My peers.

My fellows in magery.

And my very first student.

I might have lost my magic, but I hadn't lost my place in their world after all.

Then the closest troll — a troll I thought I recognized from my first day here — turned and lifted one foot high behind Lord Ihlmere.

A beam of white light flashed out from the elf's hands ...

...And that massive foot stepped down on him with a bone-splitting **CRUNCH.**

I swallowed down bile as the white light vanished, quenched at the same moment as its owner.

A sigh rippled through the company of elves. I heard retching noises from a few of the humans around me.

The elven king looked on calmly as the troll stepped back, leaving a crumpled white pile before him on the snowy ground.

"*Rest in peace, my old enemy,*" the king said in ancient Densk.

Then he looked up with a cool, diplomatic smile.

"Well," he said to Lady Cosgrave in perfect Anglish. "Shall we begin our ceremony?"

15

The rest of the ceremony passed without incident. As the clouds above us gradually parted and the snowfall outside our bubble slowed from a thick flurry to a mist, the representatives of the Boudiccate and the elven court traded and received their traditional greetings and reassurances in the sing-song tones of ancient ritual.

When the solstice sun hit its highest point, shining weakly from a pale blue sky, the very last snowflakes fell with a sigh outside our protected gathering.

The storm was over at long last.

"May we tempt Your Majesty to stay and join us for a Solstice Feast?" Lady Cosgrave asked at the very end, as the elves stepped back to take their leave. "It may not measure up to the famous delicacies of your own court, but..."

"We thank you," said the elven king, "but we must return. It has been too long since we partook of a great hunt." His silver eyes glittered as he spoke those words, and a hiss of anticipation sounded from his gathered courtiers.

It sparked something primeval in my spine — something that remembered a time, not so long ago, when humans had been favored elven prey.

I fought the sudden, cowardly urge to sidle backwards.

The elven king's icy gaze passed over our assembled company and landed with the weight of inevitability upon me. "There is," he murmured, "still the question of a new ambassadress from your nation. Perhaps we might finally agree upon one who is accustomed to speaking freely to elves ... and understanding our own words even in the most perilous of circumstances."

My stomach clenched.

"Why, yes," said Lady Cosgrave brightly, taking another step toward him. "In fact, my own young cousin, Miss Fennell, has developed quite an interest in your court, as you may have gathered from her earlier contributions! She would make an excellent addition to your company. Or —"

"Forgive me, ma'am." Miss Fennell gave an apologetic smile to her cousin and a deep, respectful bow to the elven king. "Under other circumstances, I would be honored beyond words by such an appointment ... but I'm afraid I'm rather urgently needed here at the moment."

Her hand closed around Miss Banks's arm, and the two of them leaned into each other in a moment of perfect harmony.

But I couldn't enjoy it even for their sake as the elven king's lips curved into a smile of dangerous satisfaction ... and his gaze remained firmly fixed on me.

"I am no diplomat." My voice came out half-strangled. "I would be a terrible ambassadress, Your Highness."

"And yet," purred the elven king, "I do see why Lord Ihlmere found you intriguing." His eyes narrowed, and his voice dropped to a silken croon that tugged underneath my skin. "You've lost your own magic, haven't you? I can see it locked into your bones, unreachable ... at least, as long as you remain in this outer world." His smile deepened. "Our magic works differently than yours, you know ... and so do the forces of nature within our hills. If you tasted the mysteries of our hidden court, you might yet be surprised by what possibilities you could discover ... but only while you remained with us."

My magic. The possibility shot through me like a jolt of lightning, every inch of me from the nape of my neck to my gloved fingertips suddenly tingling with alertness.

It was the impossible dream that had consumed me for the last four months, even after I'd told myself that I had given up hope. It was the single, overriding goal that I had spent my entire life fighting to achieve.

I could almost taste the power flowing through me once again. It was so amazing — so miraculous — I felt a sob of pure wonder try to break its way out from my throat.

I'd have to give up everything to achieve it — but when had I not happily sacrificed everything else in my life for the pursuit of magic?

As my head whirled, I wrenched my gaze away from the elven king, taking one last look at the human semicircles around me before I gave my answer.

Amy's eyes were huge with shock, but her lips curved into a wobbling smile as I met her gaze, and her chin dipped into a tiny nod of acceptance.

Jonathan frowned, folding his arms across his chest, but he didn't speak.

Wrexham's dark eyes held all his heart ... and then he took a deep, shuddering breath and took a firm step backwards, away from me.

...Letting me go at last.

My family and my lover had always allowed me to make

my own choices in the end. And I had never hidden from anyone in my life the truth of where my priorities lay.

So I stood on my own for the first time that day as I gave the elven king a deep and heartfelt bow. "I am truly honored by your invitation, Your Majesty," I said, "but I cannot — no," I corrected myself firmly, "I *will* not accept it."

I wouldn't use anyone else as a shield for me this time. This was my decision, mine alone, and my moment: the moment, after all those months of pain and despair, to finally step away for good from the wreckage of my past dreams and stride into a new and different future.

I'd thought I'd lost everything four months ago. But in the months since then, I'd discovered even deeper priorities after all ... and shining new possibilities.

The elven king's eyebrows rose. The elf-lords around him stiffened.

"I have important work to do here," I explained, keeping my chin raised and my gaze unyielding, "and people I love far too dearly to leave behind."

"Ah." The elven king let out a hissing sigh and gave an infinitesimal shrug. "A pity, that. But if the Boudiccate has no other appropriate candidates to suggest..."

"Ahem." Standing in the inner semicircle, old Mrs. Seabury planted her walking stick in the snow before her like a statement of its own. "Your Majesty." Her wrinkled brown face creased into a wicked smile. "I believe you'll find I can speak *my* mind ... and I have a reasonable understanding, too."

"Why, Mrs. Seabury." The king's face lit into a startlingly open and amused smile of his own. "Our old nemesis. You always did know how to speak your truths, didn't you?"

She'd been the oldest member of the Boudiccate for as long as I could remember ... but for an instant, as Mrs.

Seabury grinned at the elven king, I could almost see the fiercely sparkling young woman she had once been.

...A woman who, perhaps, had not been as different from myself as I'd always imagined.

"We would," said the elven king, "be honored indeed to welcome you into our ancient halls. And we shall expect you to join us there by the next moonfall at the latest." He bowed, with deep respect, and turned away. "*To the hunt*."

A chorus of eerie beauty answered him as every elf-lord spoke as one. "*The hunt*!"

Snow swept upwards from the ground to surround them ...

And they were gone, leaving the rest of us behind in a cold, clear day.

My limbs were suddenly trembling in long, shivering waves. Laughter and tears crowded together in my throat, until it was impossible to distinguish between them.

The magical bubble around us disappeared with a snap. "No need for *that* anymore!" Lord Cosgrave dusted off his hands. Letting out a puff of disbelieving laughter, he shook his head. "Well ... well. Indeed." He turned to his wife. "Now to the feast?"

"Now to the feast," Lady Cosgrave agreed in a shaking voice. She rested one hand on his arm for a long, shuddering moment before straightening and assuming her usual regal demeanor. "And then ... then we all have much to discuss. Including..." She gave Mrs. Seabury an exasperated look. "A new member of the Boudiccate to appoint on extremely short notice, *apparently*, as we're being abandoned by our oldest member."

"Ha!" Mrs. Seabury snorted and turned toward the house, waving her walking stick for emphasis. "A fine muck you'll all make of it without me, I wager! But I've no time for this nonsense. I'm off to eat!"

A new member of the Boudiccate. My gaze flew to my sister-in-law.

But at this utterly crucial political moment, she was, for once, ignoring all of her friends and colleagues to hurry toward me across the snow. "*Cassandra.*" Amy flung her arms around me, her firm, rounded belly pressing hard against mine. "Cassandra, you sweet, absurd fool. You could have reclaimed your magic after all! How could you say no to that?"

I pressed my cheek into her soft, crinkly dark hair, breathing deeply as the last waves of shock and fear and regret and relief shivered through me, leaving me emptied out ... and finally free.

"I have everything I need right here," I whispered.

Something hit me hard in the stomach, and I jerked backward. "What —?!"

Amy's eyes brimmed with tears, but she beamed as she rested one hand on her belly. "Apparently, your niece wanted to be a part of this conversation."

A choke of laughter escaped my throat as I took that in.

My niece ... whom I would actually meet, myself, in person, after all.

A new generation was unmistakably beginning.

Jonathan grabbed me for a rough hug, mussing up my hair. "Don't worry," he growled, "she'll meet you soon enough. And then we'll have *two* lots of trouble in this family!"

"Oh —!" I shoved him off, grinning. "I was never the troublesome one in *our* family. If you only remembered..."

But the words dried up in my throat as the semicircles parted and Wrexham strode toward me at a near-run, tall and lean and full of so much focused intensity — all for me, forever, after all — that I didn't even try to stop myself.

In full view of the assembled members of the Boudiccate and every magician in the house-party, I lunged forward and threw myself directly at him.

His lips were cold and perfect. His arms locked me close ... and *home*, for the rest of our lives, after all.

"*Hopelessly* compromised," I heard Jonathan say behind me, with satisfaction. "I daresay they'll have to get married *this week* to make up for the shame of it!"

But I had far more important things to rise to than my brother's teasing.

When Wrexham finally pulled back, he kept his firm hands around my waist and grinned down at me, his lean, dark face alight with unleashed happiness. "'Important work,' eh?" he asked.

Most of the Boudiccate had disappeared by then. The magicians were still milling around, of course, discussing various details of the near-confrontation with an inordinate amount of hand-waving and noisy debate over *exactly* which spells would have worked best if they'd only been called for...

...but I ignored them all to grin up at my fiancé with pure joy.

"I do," I said. "I've finally found a new vocation to replace my first one."

It was true.

Nothing would ever be quite the same as practicing magic myself ... but I'd finally realized that there was one moment in the past week, after all, when I'd felt every bit as deep a satisfaction as I ever had when casting a spell ... along with that singular feeling that I'd thought I'd lost forever: the certainty that *this* was what I was meant from birth to do.

Generations were shifting, and not only in my family. It was time for my own goals to shift, too.

"Oh, really?" Wrexham cocked one eyebrow. He'd been watching me ever since we first met, and I'd been watching him, too — so I knew exactly that look of sizzling anticipation in his face. It meant he thought he had puzzled out the answer to a particularly tricky problem before I had.

Ha.

His smirk of satisfaction confirmed it. "It's young Miss Banks," he said, "isn't it? You've come up with a new strategy to get her into the Great Library, along with all of those other young women like her."

"Not anymore." I shook my head without regret. "Amy was right," I admitted. "There would be *so* much resistance to that from the Great Library, the Boudiccate and more. I would need to spend all of my days playing politics, and it would *still* take years for the Great Library to finally fling their doors open. That's far too long for the girls who need training *now* ... and I was never meant to be a politician."

For once, that thought didn't even make me grimace. I knew exactly who I was, now, and I no longer needed confirmation from anyone else to believe it.

"I am a magician," I said firmly, "and you were right: losing the ability to practice my magic didn't take away any of my knowledge from the last twenty years of study. So..." I looked around, including my brother and sister-in-law in my gaze as they stepped up beside us, a warm circle of family and support that I knew I would be able to count on forever.

"What would you all think," I asked, "if I started a new school of my own?"

Jonathan's bushy eyebrows shot upward. "A magic school, you mean? For girls? As an alternative to the Great Library?"

Not an alternative, I thought with deep satisfaction. *A competitor.*

If the Great Library wouldn't hire a woman or train any others ... then as much as I'd adored my own time there, it was time to shake them out of their complacency for good. Let them try to ignore a whole generation of fabulous new female magicians!

But there was time enough to reveal all the details of my plan later. In the meantime, I smiled at my brother as I pulled out the final card that I knew would convince him.

"I'd like to add another subject to the curriculum," I told him. "The Great Library may not require it for their own students, but *I* think this adventure has proven quite conclusively that magic alone isn't enough for a working magician in the field. No, *my* students will need a good understanding of—"

"History!" Jonathan finished in a crow of triumph. "Good God, if you only knew how many times I'd tried to tell hard-headed magicians — oh, and I know *exactly* where you ought to start! If I can just..."

I turned to his wife as Jonathan began to rummage through the inner pockets of his coat. "Of course, there is still the question of where to host my school," I told her. "I could rent a house somewhere, I suppose, if I found somewhere secluded that I could afford, or..."

"Away from us? Don't be absurd! If you're going to do this, you'll need our help. And if you think we're going to lose you all over again...!" Amy's brown eyes narrowed. I could almost see the wheels of strategy beginning to turn inside her head as she tapped one finger against her side.

"We do have an unused dower house on the estate. That should be large enough at least for the first lot of students ... and then perhaps..."

My sister-in-law's words trailed off as her pretty face tightened into the look of intense concentration that heralded a perfect political maneuver in the making. Beside her, Jonathan pulled out a commonplace book to start scribbling down notes with a silver pencil, muttering to himself all the while.

My family was on my side, as always — and together, we were unstoppable.

"So?" Keeping my hands wrapped firmly around his shoulders, I looked up challengingly at Wrexham, the only one who hadn't spoken yet. "What do *you* think of my great plan? Are you still ready and willing to marry me even if I scandalize all of your colleagues and the Boudiccate itself?"

Wrexham's smile was slow and certain as he pulled me even closer into the warmth of his embrace. "I think, Harwood," said the love of my life with deep affection, "that you live to scandalize the nation ... and I can't wait to be a part of it."

"You always will be," I promised him.

Magic swirled through the air around us as the other magicians' loud debate turned into a laughing, cheering competition.

Sparks and flares danced in the corner of my vision.

I'd spent so much of my life fighting to win every magical contest that I came across...

But now I closed my eyes, smiling, and kissed my fiancé, while grand plans and schemes built themselves in my head and happiness soared irresistibly through my body.

For the first time in months, I couldn't wait to see what the future would bring me.

WHAT COMES NEXT

Thank you so much to everyone who's read this first volume in Cassandra's story! Volume II, *Thornbound,* will be published sometime in 2018. To find out the details as soon as possible — and to get access to free tie-in short stories and giveaways! — please sign up to my newsletter now: www.stephanieburgis.com/newsletter

If you have the time and energy to review *Snowspelled* on Amazon, Goodreads or elsewhere, I would be incredibly grateful. Word-of-mouth makes a huge difference, especially with a new series. Thank you!

ACKNOWLEDGMENTS

Thank you so much to all of the fearless beta-readers who read first-draft chapters of this story as I wrote them and cheered me along through moments of despair: Aliette de Bodard, Rene Sears, Jenn Reese, Tiffany Trent, Patrick Samphire and David Burgis. I appreciate you all so much!

Thanks to Leesha Hannigan for the gorgeous cover art, and thanks to Patrick Samphire for the wonderful cover design! Thanks also to Patrick Samphire for patiently helping me with so many aspects of creating this book.

I am so grateful to everyone who critiqued part or all of this novella: Laura Florand, Patrick Samphire, Rene Sears, Molly Ker Hawn, and Amber Lough.

I owe an enormous amount to everyone who carefully proofread the manuscript for me: Rich Burgis, Sophie Anderson, Karen Bultiauw, Anne Nesbet, Deva Fagan, Nancy Palmer, Susan Franzblau, Bridgit Boggs, and R.J. Anderson. You guys all deserve so much chocolate! Any mistakes that still appear here are all my fault — but there are *far* fewer of them because of you.

And oh, I owe so many thanks to everyone who patiently

critiqued one or more of my *infinite* variations on a blurb for this book: Jenn Reese, Rene Sears, Tiffany Trent, Aliette de Bodard, Leah Cypess, Jackie Dolamore, Claire Fayers, Jaime Lee Moyer, Tricia Sullivan, Deva Fagan, Ben Burgis, David Burgis and Patrick Samphire. Thank you guys!

And for inspiration: thank you SO MUCH to Vickie Ruggiero, who founded our Skype Book Club and inspired me to write exactly the kind of novella that would make both of us happy. I wanted this story to be fun to discuss with a good friend. I hope that I've succeeded!

Most of all, thank you so much to the readers who've followed me through multiple genres and adventures. I appreciate you guys so much!

ABOUT THE AUTHOR

Stephanie Burgis has lived in Michigan, Vienna, and Yorkshire, and now lives in Wales, surrounded by castles and coffee shops, with her husband (fellow writer Patrick Samphire), their two children, their (very) vocal tabby cat, and thousands of books. She is the author of two historical fantasy novels for adults, *Masks and Shadows* and *Congress of Secrets* (both published by Pyr Books), as well as four MG fantasy novels, most recently *The Dragon with a Chocolate Heart* (published by Bloomsbury in 2017).

Her MG novel *The Dragon with a Chocolate Heart* was named one of the Best New Children's Books Summer 2017 by *The Guardian*, her adult novel *Masks and Shadows* was included in Locus Magazine's Recommended Reading List for 2016, and her first MG novel, *Kat, Incorrigible*, won the Waverton Good Reads Award for Best Début Children's Novel by a British Author.

You can read more about her and her books and short stories on her website: www.stephanieburgis.com and sign up for her newsletter for free tie-in short stories and news.

CPSIA information can be obtained
at www.ICGtesting.com
Printed in the USA
LVOW12s1742041017
551169LV00001B/44/P